Canada Geese and Apple Chatney

stories by

Sasenarine Persaud

TSAR
Toronto
1998

We acknowledge the support of the Canada Council for the Arts for our publishing program. We also acknowledge support from the Ontario Arts Council.

Cover Art: *Out of the Valley* ©1996 Brent Townsend ©1996 The Greenwich Workshop®, Inc. Courtesy of The Greenwich Workshop, Inc., Shelton, CT

For information on the limited edition fine art prints by Brent Townsend call 1-800-577-0666.

Canadian Cataloguing in Publication Data

Persaud, Sasenarine, 1958-
    Canada geese and apple chatney : stories

ISBN 0-920661-72-6

I. Title.
PS8581.E7495C36 1998   C813'.54   C98-932675-6
PR9199.3.P47C36 1998

Printed in Canada by Coach House Printing.

TSAR Publications
P. O. Box 6996, Station A
Toronto, Ontario M5W 1X7
Canada

Memory, verily, is more than space. Therefore, even if many not possessing memory should be assembled; indeed they would not hear any one at all, they would not think, they would not understand . . .

Chandogya Upanishad (VII.xii.1)

CONTENTS

Part One

The Dog

My great grandfather was a Kashmiri Brahmin. So my *Aja* said. My *Aja*, my father's father, said that his father while still a little boy in India had been selected from all the Brahmin boys in the district for training as a purohit, a special priest. He was trained in *Tantra*, among other disciplines. *Tantra*, that murky set of philosophical beliefs and practices which many claim comprise the controversial and occasionally disputed *fifth Veda*, deals with the manipulation of physical laws which some call *jadu*, magic, and with the physical bodies of male and female in such a way that divine union is achieved.

What was, and has always been, fascinating for me about my *Aja's* stories about his father was the manner in which my great grandfather was selected. All the eligible Brahmin boys were stripped and minutely examined for marks, moles, scratches on their bodies, the presence of which automatically disqualified them for this special training. My great grandfather was chosen, he was among the purest of the pure and he was proud of this and so was my *Aja*. Fanaticism with purity and cleanliness has been a hallmark of these Kashmiri Brahmins. He said—my *Aja*—that his mother was a Kashmiri Brahmini and she was the fairest of the fair—"whiter than milk, black hair, green eyes. There was nobody more tender than she—and more beautiful."

Growing up, my *Aja* said, they ate no meat, or fish, or even eggs.

But times, and even places, change. The 1857 mutiny in India came and my *Aja's Aja* who had moved closer to Delhi and who was in some way connected to the new Indian army—the Indian Indian army—felt it was safest if my great grandfather and his wife were spirited out of the country. The British had called in reinforcements from throughout the British Empire and the Sikhs were already fighting with the British against the Indian army, against Indian independence. Stories of atrocities by the British side—murder, rape—were rampant and not untrue. And so my *Aja* came to be born in British Guiana in South America and not in Mother India, not in the sacred, pure Bhaarat. He never forgave the British for this, nor the Sikhs. And so from India to British Guiana, to independent Guyana, to Canada . . . What happened to my *Aja's Aja* after the mutiny was put down, nobody knows for certain. It is presumed that he and those with him—women and children—were executed and the bodies dumped into mass graves.

But some things never change. That certain Brahminical obsession, even fanaticism, about cleanliness and purity, has surfaced in a curious way. When I first came to Canada I was shocked at the way Canadians carried their dogs, treated them as though they were gods—while often dismissing other humans. I couldn't get over my shock and amazement when for the first time on a Toronto city street I saw a young woman put her hand in a transparent plastic bag and pick up dog shit from the pave. There was almost a look of pleasure on her face as she picked up her dog, stroked it, and hurried back home. I know all the arguments concerning pets—but these meant nothing to me. For days I felt repulsed at the thought, and whenever I sat next to a "white" woman in a bus or on the subway I felt myself edging away, thinking, "Does she have a dog or cat, a pet? Did she just cuddle it, did she just pick up dog shit or cat shit, did she wash her hands or face or pet-rubbed clothes?"

One day last week, a woman came to my desk to make an inquiry about her mortgage payments. As she sat down, she put her tiny dog on my desk.

"Get your dog off my desk," I shouted, standing up violently, "Please!" I added, realizing how rude I must have sounded. Everyone else in the bank was looking at me and the manager came out of his office and apologized to the woman. The woman wanted an apology from me. I told her when she apologized for dumping her dog on my desk I would apologize. She didn't and I didn't, not even when the manager called me into his office and cautioned me about the repercussions of my behaviour, the effects on my career, the customer coming first and so on. I was fed up with dancing to the whims and fancies of "the customer." Did customers forget that I too was a human being, that I deserved to be treated with the dignity and decency they seemed to lose once they became "customers"? I told the manager he could fire me, but I was not going to apologize until I got an apology from the client . . .

That incident has caused me a lot of soul-searching. Do I hate pets, animals, dogs . . .? Was human life more important than any other form of life . . .? Where did the paths of Mahavira, Buddha and Brahmins travel together and diverge . . . ?

From as far back as my memory will take me, we had a dog. We called him Brownie because of his hair, which was mostly golden brown. His underside was white, the area from his nose to his eyes was white and part of his tail was white, but these were lost in his golden brown. I can hear those calls now every day at dusk, "Brownie, Brownie, Brownie, Brownieee . . ." just before we had our dinner. These were always made at the top of our voices as Brownie might be anywhere—next door, at the end of the street, in the alley, even in the next street. We loved to have our voices carried on the wind, mingling with the birdsongs and treesongs—to the end of the earth. And every boy in the neighbourhood—throughout Guyana, I later found out, at least in the Indian areas—used exactly the same intonation of voice and pitch, the same poetry of sound in calling for the family dog. Sometimes adults called the dogs too, the husbands and fathers, but rarely a female. Whether the dog was called Blackie, Whitie, Tarzan, Jimmy, Tiger the

5

same sequence and rhythm would sound out at dusk.

I think our dogs used to like the calls and wait for them, because they knew full well that as soon as it started to get dark it would be time for dinner. They could well have saved us the calls as no sooner did we make a call or two than they would come bounding out of the dusk, happy and wagging their tails as though we had not seen each other for years. So it was with Brownie. One day I called and called and Brownie did not come home and I wanted to cry and everyone came and stood with me on our platform, and we all called but Brownie did not come. My father went down the stairs and out onto our bridge and on the road and he too called, but still there was no Brownie. I started to cry, not because I felt that something had happened to Brownie, but because I felt I had failed our family, that I had failed in an important, a very important event in our lives. Brownie had never failed to answer before—and it had to happen when it was my evening to call. I think we all knew that Brownie was safe, we had great confidence in his ability to take care of himself, we felt that he was as intelligent as us and most humans. Of this we were somewhat proud. That evening everybody came and sat with me on our platform and we waited, taking turns calling.

It must have been almost an hour later when Brownie came bounding up the stairs. He headed straight for my mother. It was dark but we could see the gashes all over his body and the blood. A pack of dogs must have attacked Brownie in some distant street, and alone and far away from home, he didn't run, he stood his ground and fought, though he must have known what the outcome would be. My mother must have cried a little that night. I think we all did, visibly or otherwise, but it was dark and who could be certain? My mother went inside and came back with her bottle of "dye lotion" which she used to put on all our cuts and bruises and which burned but disinfected our wounds. Using a clean, new strip of white cotton cloth she cleaned and washed Brownie's wounds while we held him still. He made soft whining sounds. My mother made bandages of clean, white cotton for the larger wounds on his hind legs and back. And in her precise, analytical way she commented,

"It is one-a'dhe principles of our *Dharma*—to do our duty whatever it is, wherever it is regardless a-dhe odds, even if we feel we'll lose is not important. Gandhiji says 'cowardice is impotence worse than violence . . .' It is better to fight knowing you may lose, or will lose dhan to be a coward and run away . . . Run away, but fight first. Dhat way you get a measure a-yuh strength against dhe enemy so when you go back yuh-know when to go back and where, and yuh shake dhe enemy's belief dhat because he look so strong yuh gun neva attack he. An despite he strength he always worrying when yuh gun strike . . ."

Brownie, who was huddled on the platform outside the back door almost in the centre of us, seemed to have understood every word perfectly well. And because of what my mother said I felt good then about Brownie's battle. And proud. I think if the society and time had permitted, and if she wanted to be one, my mother would have made a great general. Brownie lay there and smiled and wagged his tail. Those of us who have lived closely to animals know that they smile, and laugh and cry and communicate in their own ways with great eloquence. For weeks afterwards Brownie did not leave our yard. I believe he loved the extra attention he got because he was "sick," like all patients, and like good and caring relatives we loved giving him the extra attention. When his wounds were healed you would never believe he had been in a fight. His body did not show even the slightest trace of a scar. He started going out again and we commenced our routine. "Brownie, Brownie, Brownie, Brownieee . . . ," we would call in the lovely dusks. He always took longer to return and when he did, he came with a majesty and a swagger (and occasionally with a slight limp, a little blood on his body) which suggested a victorious fight. This lasted for about two weeks. After this he would come bounding for his dinner, as usual, after the first or second call. We figured that in the two weeks following his recuperation he had been "taking out" his enemies, members of the group that had attacked him, one by one, or in twos.

For people not familiar with that world some things may seem strange, but I point out that in some ways it was a more humane world. Firstly, for us a dog was a German Shepherd, an Alsatian, a Doberman, the "common dog"—a cross between these three, and other dogs with various percentages and strains from these others. I had never seen in the flesh those little shrimps of dogs until I came to Canada—poodles, spaniels, adult dogs no larger than, for us, a normal puppy, and even now I find it difficult to think of them as dogs. My friends in the old country would laugh and laugh on seeing one. But as Shakespeare said, there are dogs and dogs . . .

Dogs, of course, were pets but not pets first. Dogs were guards first, protectors. When everybody went to work or school the dog looked after the house, and where the wife and kids were at home, the dog sounded the alarm at the approach of a stranger, and if the stranger was so imprudent as to enter a yard without the consent of master or mistress he was expected to be chased and bitten by the dog. A sign on a gate which announced BEWARE OF DOG meant just that. Our gate had such a sign prominently displayed. And at nights the dog was master of the yard, he ensured his masters got a good night's rest. Brownie did that too. No stranger would dare enter our yard. Despite all of this, a dog never dwelled inside a house with its keepers, indeed, rarely entered. The dog roamed the streets, the parapets, the alleys and so could not enter the house of a human. That would be unclean and unhygienic. For that reason too, nobody entered his house or somebody else's house with his shoes on. Shoes were left outside the door—this was especially so in Indian homes, a fixed and unbreakable rule. We were aware that in other homes this was not always observed, but in a society where by far Indians made up the largest ethnic group and formed the majority of the population, this practice unobtrusively, like other Indian practices, gained unconscious acceptance in the larger society. Even here in Canada, I note many Indians never proceed much further than their doors with their shoes. It is, I believe, important to understand all of these things in order to understand the treatment of dogs in that society and why I feel that, despite the seem-

ing distance and aloofness towards dogs, people there are very kind to
their dogs.

So Brownie never entered our house. The stairs and the mats on the
back platform and the front verandah were as far as he got, and he
knew that. He would occasionally poke his nose and head in the back
door when my mother was cooking something—and when we were
all at home both doors would be open during the day, if it were not
raining—but he would not enter the house.

Some people had kennels for their dogs, and leashes. But by and
large most dogs made their beds on platforms or verandahs or under
the house, that is, on the unbarricaded portion of the ground floor
(which most of the time was the entire ground floor) or a combination
of all three, which was the case with Brownie. As regards leashes, it
was a sign of good breeding if a dog did not require one, no matter
how fierce, and we never had one for Brownie. Dogs enjoyed a kind
of freedom. During certain times they roamed at will. Brownie would
stay at home all day but as soon as my father and mother came home,
he would disappear until we called him for his dinner. And his dinner
was whatever we were having for dinner—there was almost no difference between dog food and human food. Some people did go to the
butcher and buy scraps for their dogs. Once or twice, some time before
I was born, my father had gone to get meat for Brownie —it was felt
that dogs should be pampered with raw meat to make them fiercer—
but Brownie would have none of this. He was not a meat eater and
had, it turned out, a certain Brahminical distaste for meat eating. And
this was what made Brownie special in our household, in our street
and neighbourhood and much further afield. Brownie was the pride of
all of our relatives and friends because of his "Indianness."

I have mentioned earlier that my great grandfather had been a Kashmiri Brahmin and his wife, my great grandmother, a Kashmiri
Brahmini who ate no flesh or eggs, but time and place had changed.
My *Aja,* my father's father, did not eat flesh, eggs or shrimp, but he
was not so strict with my father and though none of it was cooked in
the home, my grandparents silently allowed my father to eat chicken

and duck at the homes of various other friends and relatives as they knew that he had no *panditai* aspirations. Other Brahmins in British Guiana were known to indulge in eating chicken and fish occasionally, and this was frowned upon. The "Bengali Babus" were known to be fond of fish—I believed some Bengali Brahmin had said, in all earnestness, as a defence, that fish and shrimp were the "vegetables of the sea." Although there was a laxness among Indians, Brahmins who were pandits were expected to confirm to a strict vegetarian diet. The Bengali Brahmins who were pandits soon found that nobody asked them to perform *pujas* once it was known that they ate fish. Strict caste observances became a rarity. When my father married and moved to his own home, he had my mother cook chicken, fish and other meats for him though she herself did not eat any of it. My *Aja* was very displeased with this and it was one of the reasons he rarely ever visited our home, though he liked my mother very much.

My mother could pass for a Kashmiri Brahmini—for the Kashmiri Brahmini my *Aja's* mother was "whiter than milk, black hair . . ."—but her eyes were cane-juice-brown. My *Aja* liked my mother's "purity and cleanliness" and her concern for family and family tradition though he himself had let a lot of that tradition slip by. I believe my mother was proud of marrying into my father's family with its "clean" Brahminism going back to my great grandfather and beyond—not that my father did not have his own desirability. At the time of his marriage, my father was charming and quite debonair. His cinematic flashiness came from Hollywood and Bombay jointly, and while Clarke Gable made quite an impression on him and the young men of his generation, I think he fell more under the spell of Raj Kapoor, Dilip Kumar and Mukesh. This I believe affected my mother favourably, but also my father being a Hindi scholar and knowing Sanskrit, in addition to his family history, must have had a great effect on her—not that it really mattered when it came to getting married. My parents did not have much say about their marriage. My father's parents and my mother's parents made a match. My parents could only say no or yes. If for some reason an answer was no, another match was sought.

One did not disobey one's parents easily, but one of my mother's sisters had in fact said no to a match, and so had my father.

My father's meat-eating had greatly disappointed my mother. She felt my father was wrong to deviate from the sacred trust of his ancestors and when Brownie refused to eat meat, she felt it was a sure sign that my father was wrong. My father was unmoved. Shortly after I was born, they found when I could eat cooked food that anything containing any meat or eggs caused rashes on my skin. My father did not stop his meat eating but toned it down considerably, restricting himself and my brothers and sisters to fish, shrimps or chicken occasionally. In me, my mother felt justified and to some extent fulfilled and so did my *Aja*. I became his favourite.

But Brownie became the favourite of all favourites and nobody begrudged him that. Brownie would know by some extraordinary way which days my mother fasted and he fasted too. He ate only when my mother broke her fast. This was the most fascinating thing about Brownie, apart from his strictly vegetarian diet. And often I have wondered over the years, like many of the adults at that time, which extraordinary Yogi or Brahmin had done some terrible deed to be reborn as our Brownie to be cleansed of his bad karma. The cynics will no doubt have a good laugh at this thought, but today it is generally accepted that there is life before birth; and we who have known for centuries that this is part of the parcel of life after death because we have been there and back, know that in time this too will be accepted. But there was more yet to Brownie. When my mother came home from *mandir* on Sundays or on *parab* days Brownie waited for his bit of the sacred *prasad*. Often when we all went to *mandir* there was no keeping him home. He would trot after us and sit attentively just outside the *mandir* doors until the *puja* was finished and we came out. At first nobody liked the idea because he looked so fierce in his almost Yogi-like attention, but by and by people accepted his presence and later were glad for it. Whenever he was around nobody lost footwear left outside the *mandir* door.

Three days before my mother died, I must have been about ten at the time, Brownie would not go out of the yard but kept patrolling its perimeter, and looking up to the sky and growling. In the nights he kept barking at the sky and when my father went to check to see if there was any prowler around, he found no one. The day before she died, Brownie became less active and came quietly and lay all day on the mat on the back platform just outside the door. The next day, Sunday, would be *Shivratri*, the day we would observe the coming down from *Kailash* of *Shiva*, the lord of the universe, the *Nataraja* consumed in his eternal dance of life and death. For us it was a special day as our ancestors had been Shaivites, devotees of *Shiva*, and my great grandfather had special training in *Tantra* often associated with *Shiva* worship. My mother cleaned and cooked all of the day before and Brownie just lay on the mat outside the kitchen door keeping her company. She occasionally repeated to him, "Cheer up boy, tomorrow is a big day." He wagged his tail slowly and kept sniffing the air.

I remember the Sunday my mother died very distinctly. There are some things one never forgets, and this for me is one of these. I had got up early and gone downstairs. What I saw made me want to cry without knowing why. Brownie lay on the ground just underneath my parents' room and he was still. He did not move as he would normally, bounding up and wagging his tail, dancing around us in a morning greeting. I went over to him thinking something was wrong with him. I saw the brief flicker of his eyes and knew he was alive, but his eyes were the saddest eyes I have ever seen in my life. Tears had caked at the edges of both eyes and even as I looked at him, more tears trickled down the sides of his eyes. I too wanted to cry but I just bent down and put my hand on his head, and he made such a quiet and soulful moan that I sat on the ground, in the dust, next to him and he snuggled up to me. I put my arm around him. It was the first and only time I have ever had such physical contact with Brownie.

You have to understand that for me, for most Indians I have known, a touch is an act of the highest and deepest physical intimacy, a very spiritual action. Nothing physical is more sacred than touch, and touching is an act that does not come easily to us, perhaps because we are so emotional a people. I often wonder at this in Canadian society where touching seems to mean nothing. In the office the girls, all of whom were born and grew up here, often put their arms around me or the manager as though this is of no consequence. Even occasionally, moving around the office our bodies would brush. For me each time this happens electricity shoots through my body, envelops it, and heightens sensuality despite all my discipline and yoga. I try my best to avoid physical contact, because for me one only touches a woman or person one has deep feelings or reverence for, and one allows one-self to be touched only by someone who has such deep feelings or reverence for one. To touch is to communicate many currents which cannot be communicated by speech and so too, to look eye through eye is an act of communication, of expressing things which cannot be expressed in speech or writing. To touch here is like to eat, to breathe—unconscious acts, acts without importance, acts which are done because they are done, have always been done as part of, as a relatively unimportant part of, other unimportant things. And so in the crowded subways and buses, buttocks touch buttocks, thighs thighs, breasts shoulders and occasionally fingers find themselves flung into far fetched meaningless corners of flesh—dead human flesh. I hate the crowded subways and the crowded buses for the touch, that touch . . .

That morning so long ago I sat in the dust with my arm around Brownie and his head in my lap. I must have been crying too when my brothers came downstairs. When the neighbours and the other people came, Brownie was still cradled in my lap. I believe it was only my father who was able to get me up from the dust and to relinquish my hold on Brownie. In the nights that followed my mother's death—the autopsy showed just the slightest trace of cardiac arrest and the doc-tors felt it was as though she just left her body willingly: my father claimed he felt nothing, heard no cry from her and he was a light sleeper; when he woke up that morning, she was lying on her back beside him, one hand on her waist and the other touching his thigh. Brownie pawed at the air and pawed at the ground, fought with the dark night and growled and moaned. He was never the same after the cremation. He went around the pyre after my father, and in front of us, as though he was the eldest son of my mother—and perhaps he was. And when it was time to light the pyre, I believed he would have done it if he could, and yet in a strange way he did. While I took the lit stick and was putting it to the pyre, he came and rested his forepaws on my arm—his "hands" on my arm as we had done in puja when lighting the flame in the *havan khund*; one person lighting the flame for us all because it was not practically possible for all of us to do so at that time and place in the *puja*, and so we would all place one of our hands, in a symbolic gesture that we too were lighting the sacred flame, on the arm of the person lighting the *khund* . . .

Life went on. Weeks grew into months into years. Brownie seemed not to have aged but he had acquired one peculiarity—he hated the sight of dark colours. One day shortly after my mother died, one of my father's cousins came visiting with his family. He was well known to all of us and to Brownie. As he entered the yard Brownie bolted for him, and before anyone could react Brownie ripped his trousers to pieces without harming him, then wagging his tail as though he had just defeated another dog in a dogfight, strolled back to his former position under our house. The colour of the trousers he had just ripped up was black. Some weeks after this, Brownie rushed at one of our neighbours and ripped his navy blue uniform trousers to shreds without harming the man. Another day he rushed at the man who had come to read the electricity meter. The man, of African descent, was very dark skinned. I believe it was a good thing my father was home to control Brownie. Neighbours used the avenue when they wore dark clothes, instead of passing by our yard.

When I was almost fourteen, I went away for two weeks to a remote country village in the Essequibo, visiting with one of my classmates and his family. It was the kind of trip one always dreams of, the kind of paradise that is only half real, but which, once you have lived through you know you can never experience again because it is a combination of reality and unreality that is only possible because of your innocence and naivity. My classmate, Jitendra, though he had mentioned his younger sister, Jyoti (one and a half years younger than me) had not quite prepared me for her. Almost exactly ten years later she became my first wife. This I will come to shortly. But those two weeks were for me filled with wonder. I woke up in the mornings and looked over acres and acres of rice fields, and way in the background, acres and acres of coconut groves. Birdsongs woke me up just outside the windows, on the huge fruit trees caressing the house, and birdsongs put me to sleep. Outside, the sounds of the Essequibo River mingled with the sounds of the Atlantic Ocean in the background. The nights were pitch dark and the stars touchable, brilliant—insects hovered around the gas lamps and the breeze provoked the mosquitos into fits of buzzing.

Jyoti, so young and so simple—not quite so shy—charmed me from the beginning. I had fallen in love for the first, and I still believe, the only time in my life. It is not that I have not had deep feelings for women since then; but love like that, never! Convention, of course, made little contact or conversation possible during that first visit, but things have a way of happening. In the same way dogs communicate such great feelings and understanding through eyes, little gestures, little touches of souls on fingers. Both Sundays when we went to *mandir* in their little village—I felt she sang for me. She sang of Krishna and Radha. Not only Shiva danced so did Krishna when she sang—Gopala Gopala nacho Gopala/ Nacho nacho Hari Nandalallaa—Krishna, the eternal lover danced. She had such a beautiful voice and was such an accomplished harmonium player, that I felt I could listen to her all my life. But school would reopen soon and I had to leave for my own home.

I left her my heart. So much so that when I went home, I hardly bothered about Brownie's absence, which I attributed to one of his neighbourhood visits. At dinner time, I went out to the platform and before I could call out, my father who came out with me said, "Mahase, Brownie dead."

"When?" I asked, somewhat at a loss for words and emotion. It came as such a shock.

"First Sunday you gone. Kept growling at the night for two nights before, and digging holes in dhe sand around dhe yard." There was a long silence in which I heard the songs of the kiskadees and blue sakies in the trees. I noticed the bats in their thousands criss-crossing the twilight sky.

"Sunday morning we fine he deh." My father pointed to the huge neem tree in the backyard, "an we bury he deh right in dhe corner under dhe neem." He indicated a little mound just inside the back fence, under the spreading branches of the sacred neem.

"Couldn't dump him no matter—no matter I never get another dog," my father said. I didn't look at him, just at the mound and my head fell. He just put a hand on my shoulder and I felt a little squeeze. I knew he was crying inside for Brownie, and also for my mother. Silently he went inside. The general belief was that if you had a dog and it died, you never buried it. Once you did, you could never keep another dog in your life—or rather, another dog never stayed with you. My father and our neighbours had known people in their childhood who had buried dogs and had never been able to rear another dog. They had said that according to the older people, that had always been so in the folklore of dogs.

Mainly for this reason, I believe, everybody dumped their dogs in the river, in the Ocean, or in the huge black water canal which flowed past our house, parallel to our street out to the Atlantic. Callous? Perhaps. But once every three or four months the swollen, bloated body of what was once a dog would float by in the canal in front our house in various stages of disintegration; most of the times in a jute bag that once contained rice or sugar. This dumping of dead dogs in the canal was a contravention of municipal public health laws, and so it was often done in the cover of night. I can never remember an instance of anyone being caught in the act, and those of us who lived near the canal were ever vigilant since we would be hit by the stench whenever a dog got stuck in the weeds. Coming home from school, I remember, all the boys would practise their "cricket arm" on a stuck, bloated body. The bricks we threw landed with a dull thud, disturbed the flies and soon set the body moving towards the *Koker*, then out to the Atlantic again.

That Brownie was spared such indignity was a comforting thought. I was grateful to my father, and I too didn't mind if I never had another dog again.

I too would have gone against all the tradition, all the folklore, that this dog which had harboured some great soul paying for an ill deed, and which great soul had done enough *tapasya*, be spared the final humiliation of a dumping and a stoning, several stonings. We had thought that that was the end of Brownie—at any rate I thought so. Years went by and then suddenly my youngest sister, Rajini, who was three when my mother died and seven when Brownie died, had a great desire to have a dog. Anywhere we went and she saw a puppy, she would burst into tears and not want to leave it. This started to happen about three years after Brownie died. My father finally agreed for her to keep a puppy. We got a nice, chubby puppy and built—I helped my father—a nice "little house" for the puppy. Rajini was very happy. I believe we all were. We kept fussing over the puppy and bringing it milk, and checking to see it was warm and comfortable at nights. But soon it started to howl at nights and nobody could sleep. Shortly after, it stopped eating and started getting thinner and thinner. The vet. said nothing was wrong but perhaps it needed its mother. Sure enough, when we took it back the puppy thrived. We didn't have the heart to separate it from the mother again. Slowly Rajini's desire for a dog surfaced again, and this time we got a much older puppy, which had already separated from its mother. But this turned out to be such a cross puppy which kept snapping at us, that we had no choice but to give it away. Quietly, we all started to accept that perhaps the folklore was correct. There was no more talk of dogs for a long time. Seven years elapsed—and Brownie came back.

Rajini was the medium. She was in high school and an avid reader. She did very well in school and most of the time she came first in her class and fancied herself a great scholar—I had learnt somewhere along the way, that it is always best to have people learn some things on their own, and then it means something to them—so I never dampened her notion of being a great scholar. But at that time she had done quite a lot of reading and fancied herself something of an expert on dogs. We all deferred to her. This was just about the time Jyoti and I got married. We had made arrangements for living together in one household, as a family, which was not uncommon among the Indians and which, despite some bad experiences and publicity, was often beneficial all around. It was a time when the long arm of North American and European feminism had stretched across the Atlantic through many mediums; magazines, books and especially the cinema. The Indian extended family had come under extensive pressure, like most other forms of Indian practices, and most young Indian women were insisting that they would not live with their in-laws, especially not their mothers-in-law. I believe that Jyoti might have objected too if my mother were alive.

More than a year had elapsed since we got married. Jyoti had just become pregnant and she wanted the baby. This news made us all very happy, and it was just about this time that Rajini decided the time had come for us to have another dog. She was supported by Jyoti, with whom she had become very friendly. They went several places together and did many things together. We were all happy at this. My mother's death and my other sister's early marriage had left a vacuum in our house. My father had not remarried. Jyoti's presence gave the place a life and vitality it seemed to have lost, and the effect on Rajini was great. Rajini was starting to lose some of her reclusiveness—no doubt because she had felt lonely in a house full of males. There are, I suppose, some things you don't discuss with your brothers—especially if they are hardly at home. The house seemed fuller, and there was more laughter. It was in this atmosphere that Rajini asked. Who could refuse? We looked around, and finally Jyoti and Rajini saw a puppy they liked—a cross between an Alsatian and a Doberman. The head was Doberman and the flank and tail that of an Alsatian; it was a brownish black colour. The moment I saw him, I thought of Brownie and in my heart, I was hoping that we would call him Brownie even though his was a darker brown than Brownie's. We got him for next to nothing through Rai, my youngest brother, who had mentioned it to a classmate who had remarked that their slut had "dropped," and that they wanted to get rid of some of the puppies. I somehow got the impression that Rai's friend—Ramesh or Rajesh—was attracted to Rajini and Rajini to him. There seemed to be some subtle undercurrent. My father was not ecstatic, but he was not unhappy either. He had, since my mother's death, undergone a remarkable transformation. A transformation which did not occur overnight, but over a period of time. He had taken to reading the *Ramayan* in Hindi, and various other books on Indian philosophy, and he was taking a more active role in the activities of the *mandir*, occasionally teaching Hindi. He was spending more of his time meditating in his room. There was a reconciliation with my *Aja*, and the two men spent more time together. My *Aja* said lightheartedly, "Blood shows through." My father had given up meat eating, and extremes of emotion were rare with him, so he was not ecstatic when we brought the dog home. A day or two of deliberations followed, then Rajini announced that the dog would be called Shiva. Even my father showed surprise.

But Rajini held her own. For too long we had allowed ourselves to be defined by the "other world," the non-Indian world, it was time we defined our world. We could start with dog naming! Shiva was as good, better than Jimmy, Johnny, Tarzan, etc . . . Only a short while ago I had been telling them that Singer's Magician of Lublin had named his horse Shiva! My father smiled and shook his head. None of us had a response to Rajini. So the dog became Shiva. What Rajini said sounded familiar, and it was only later that evening I realized it sounded like Jyoti. The months progressed and we all fell in love with the dog Shiva, who was so much like Brownie. Indeed, whenever I looked into his eyes I saw Brownie. I saw the same love, the same compassion and the same knowledge—and I felt that his soul knew everything, its own past and its future. I wanted to talk to my father about this, or to my *Aja* but somehow the occasion was never there. Around my *Aja*, there were always other grandchildren, my other cousins with whom my *Aja* lived, and they had a certain possessiveness about him. At home, Rajini and Jyoti were always around. A conversation with my father on death and reincarnation never seemed quite the thing to talk about in their lively presence, and I didn't want to talk about death near Jyoti—her belly getting larger and larger . . .

One day my father said, "We should get rid of the dog."

There were several whats and whys.

"He acting strange."

"What yuh mean strange?" Asked Rajini testily.

"Well," my father hesitated, looking at me, and I knew in that instant that he too felt what I felt, he knew what I wanted to talk to him about. "He pawing the air, fighting with the night . . ." He might as well as have said the dog smelled of death.

"All dogs do dhat," Rajini responded.

"He digging holes," my father said very slowly.

"O—that's normal for dogs. In Essequibo dogs always digging holes in dhe sand," Jyoti said as if it was of no consequence.

"And Daddy, you say Hinduism is scientific, a way of life organized around logic and reason, not superstition . . ." Rajini added with some irony. Jyoti nodded. I could see he was about to respond and then thought better and remained silent, shrugging his shoulders almost imperceptibly. He was not pleased.

I was disturbed myself. I had not realized the dog was digging holes and pawing the air. It was what Brownie had done before my mother died. I started noting the holes, mainly in the yard around the area of my father's bedroom, and as soon as I did, I would fill them in and smooth them over so that there would not appear to be any traces of disturbance. I knew it would upset my father. I started to feel that perhaps it was making him feel that the time of his death was approaching. I knew of many stories of people who "saw their death coming" and no doubt so did my father. Some people believed it was possible, but many others, Rajini and Jyoti included, dismissed this as "pure imagination."

In the meantime Jyoti's time for delivery was getting nearer. She was excited. She wanted a boy and she was positive it would be a boy. She would put her hand on her belly and take my hand and put it there, especially when she felt movement, and say, "See, a boy—a boy, mischievous as he fadda." I felt that it would be a boy too, though I would have liked a girl. I just told her that whatever it was, I would be happy. The name would, of course, be a "book name" —a Hindu name determined by the time of birth. One beautiful sunny Sunday, my father flew into an uncharacteristic rage. The dog had dug a huge hole in the sand, not far from his bedroom. He had just looked out of his bedroom window and saw this huge hole and he flew into a rage. He rushed to the back platform, picked up a slipper and started hitting the dog with it, grinding his teeth and shouting,

"Dhis blasted daag—who dhe rass yuh want, stap digging hole in dhe blasted place, stap digging hole . . . "

Jyoti, Rajini and I were on the verandah in front and we could hear him. It annoyed me to hear him grind his teeth. I had not heard that since I was a kid and I knew he was very upset.

"Mahase stop him," my sister implored me, angry too that the dog was being thrashed, angry that I sat there and did not come to the defense of the dog.

"The poor dog cannot help itself and beating it will not stop it digging holes . . ." I could not understand why the dog just remained there and did not run away, and I felt my irritation rise with the dog for remaining there. If the dog remained there, I would be caught in the middle, and I would have to do something I hated, something I felt I would hate myself for, for the rest of my life. In seconds *Gita, Ramayan, Mahabharata*, my mother commenting on Brownie's fight with a group of other dogs, swirled through my mind. And I knew that the dog would not move, would not retaliate either, and my father would not stop, could not stop. They were bound by some ancient karmic law.

"Why don't you stop him!" Jyoti said with a quiet anger directed at me, "Rajini's right!"

I was angry. Angry with my sister and my wife for goading me into a confrontation I did not want ever to have. It is not that my father and I had never had disagreements, that we had not raised our voices in argument, but those were for causes I believed in, at a time when I was much younger and when I felt I knew the world, because I had gone to university and graduated with honours and had read so much. A time when in my ignorance I felt I knew more than my father because of this little "book learning," and that it was my duty to change him for "the better." I knew afterwards, many years afterwards, that I was wrong and that my father knew I was wrong and that he did not need me to ask forgiveness to forgive me. The dog had to do what it had to do, and he had to do what he had to do. Soon he would tire and leave the dog alone, but I could not say that to the two women near me then, who had fire in their eyes and were daring me to do something I did not believe had to be done. I could not stop myself. In as much a rage as my father, I rushed down the front stairs and to the back. At the bottom of the stairs, I glared up. The dog just crouched on the platform and took all the blows and I thought, "You blasted dog, get up and run down the stairs, get up, get up . . . and why the hell yuh beating the daag anyway . . ." My anger and frustration found focus in my father.

"Leave dhe daag alone," I screamed. Shocked, my father's arm froze as it was coming down for another blow. We glared at each other before he slammed down the slipper, turned towards the south looking momentarily at the neem. Automatically I followed his glance, and as he turned towards the door we momentarily looked at each other. There were tears in his eyes. I believe we both apologized in that glance. The dog slinked past, not looking at me and I wanted to hit him. He went up the front stairs where Jyoti and Rajini lavished him with attention and sympathy.

Around 2 PM the following Friday, Rajini called me at the office from the hospital. Jyoti had started having labour pains—prematurely. When I arrived at the hospital Rajini rushed up to me crying. She didn't have to say anything, I knew. When I went to look at Jyoti, I was horrified. There was a look of intense pain and anger on her face. It was frozen stiff. It seemed to be angry with me, with the world. It seemed to say, "Look all of you, look what you have reduced me to." It is the most anguished and bitter look I have ever seen on the face of anyone in my life, and its pain will stay with me for as long as I live: I hope I never see another such expression in my life. When she died, the baby was still kicking inside her . . . They performed a caesarean but it was too late. The baby died too. It would have been a boy.

My father had gone that morning, as he had taken to doing recently every now and again, to spend the day with my *Aja*. But he came back immediately he learned, and made all the arrangements for the cremation. I could hardly think, and more often I cried. After everything— the cremation and the *Shraad karma*, the "dead wuk," the offering of *pindas* and *mantras* to help the departed souls continue their journeys —was done, we remembered the dog. Somehow in the thirteen days, he seemed to have disappeared. After the *shraad karma*, he returned— at least, then he was noticed.

It was Rajini who said, "Let us get rid of him." There was no disagreement and someone produced a jute bag. I had thought it would have been a difficult thing, but when they called him, he came as though he knew. They almost did not have to put him in the bag. He walked straight in. I sat on the bottom of the back stair as he walked into that bag, and when we looked into each other's eyes for the eternity of that glance, I saw humility and compassion and forgiveness and apology. Sometimes one has to apologize for one's knowledge— especially when that knowledge hurts, humiliates, angers, embarrasses someone else.

We took the dog in a jute bag and emptied him on a back street near the sea wall, not very far away. We hated him for his foreknowledge and warnings. Rai said Shiva never even looked back. He sniffed the air, wagged his tail and headed out for the bushes on the Atlantic seashore. I thought of him somehow as a yogi, having completed his duty, heading back into the forest to continue his meditations. The miles of crab bush and huge trees there do look like a forest. We had often gone there with the dog. He knew the way back home and could have returned if he wanted, but he didn't. We have never kept a dog since, but now the dog haunts me. Whatever happened to him, I have often asked myself.

My girlfriend who was born here in Canada has suggested that we move in together, or get married, if living together and not being married hurts my "Indian sensibilities." We have both been married before and, I think, we both have a certain distaste for marriage, but neither marriage nor living together balks me. There is the problem of the dog. Her dwarfdog barks at me whenever I visit her. After her divorce her dog was her most faithful companion. She could cuddle him whenever she wanted—and he couldn't argue, or beat her, or be unfaithful. He couldn't demand that she do this or do that. His demands were so few! But now she has offered to give up her dog. What sacrifice! The dog senses that and barks when I visit. Soon he or I must go, that we both know.

What I don't know but constantly ask myself is: do I hate dogs—uncleanliness aside? I think not, yet I do believe I hate the dog, the soul which knows that I know something which I do not want to accept.

My Girl, This Indianness

"I have never been a father to her . . ." he said after I was finished. There was no emotion on his face. "And what good would this do her, or me?" he asked.

"I don't know. That is really a matter for you and her. I am just the go-between, the facilitator if you like."

"What do you think?" He asked. An aircraft took off from the Toronto Island Airport.

"Well Mr Hirwani, as I told you, we hope to get married—and I think this is something she has to come to terms with. The experience shattered her belief in the world as she knew it. And she is curious about you. Her curiosity's tempered with some anger and fear of rejection . . ."

"Does she know you have located me?"

"No. I spoke with her last Saturday night but I didn't tell her you had agreed to see me. I wanted to see what would come of all of this first. I didn't want to give her false hope, and besides, this is not going to be an easy decision for you."

He looked out the glass door. The patch of lake in the foreground was speckled with gulls and boats, and the early summer sun was low on the horizon in the north-west. In the moments I looked out with him onto the lake and the Islands, I fell in love with the lakescape—

that part of the lakefront. In those moments, I took back all I had said about not finding anything spectacular or breathtaking about the islands and the lake. The lake's pollution, the dirtiness of its water and the resentment of having it as a substitute for the Atlantic had all combined to cloud my feelings in the past.

"Are you only a journalist?" He asked suddenly. I had got him to agree to see me by telling him on the phone that I was a journalist, and that I was interested in the years he spent in British Guiana—the late 1950s and early 1960s—after he and his parents had come from India, and before they had moved on to Canada; in his perspective of those turbulent years in the political history of Guyana and the British West Indies, because I was working on a book on that period, and because he was an "outsider" and his opinions were more likely to be objective, his perspective different.

"No. I am a literary critic and also, perhaps, a social historian," I replied, not certain if he was talking to give himself time to digest the story I had told him or assessing me. I wanted to impress him. Whether he publicly accepted Debbie as his daughter or not would not make a difference, but I felt I owed it to her to make a good impression. Would he be assessing her—this daughter he had never known, had seen only a few times when she was a baby—on her choice of a partner?

"So you didn't lie about that eh!" He smiled. "Sooner or later one's past always catches up . . ." And with this admission then, for the first time that afternoon some of the tenseness left me. "You felt that if you had simply said that you were engaged to a young woman who was born before I got married to my present wife, and who felt she was my daughter and who wanted you to locate and discuss this with me before she came to Canada—I would not meet you . . ." It was half a statement half a question.

"Yes."

"What do you want from this?" He asked.

"Our children will be your grandchildren—it is not important to me whether you acknowledge this or not, but I too am curious about you.

And I want to be able to tell our children something about their history, their ancestry. And I think you two should meet, it would help her get on with her life—even if you both go your own ways—it will help her to get rid of that mysterious, unknown parent which has been bugging her these past few years since she knew. And aren't you curious?" I asked boldly, gesturing to the three photographs I had placed side by side on his desk.

"Yes," he nodded, looking at the pictures of Debbie, Debbie's mother, and the black and white photograph of himself he had given Debbie's mother twenty-five years ago.

"She is your daughter. There is no hiding that. She has your long straight nose, your round, dark brown eyes, your slim face, your long limbs and slimness—your complexion." The resemblance was unmistakable. He pulled the pictures closer to him. Debbie's mother had recently told her he was born in 1939 in Sindh near Karachi, but the partition of India in which most of Sindh went to the newly created Pakistan saw his Hindu family losing their entire fortune. They moved south to Bombay and started all over again; then in the early '50s his family moved yet again, this time to British Guiana following other Sindhis who had settled there, in East Africa, and in Trinidad and were doing well.

His father had set up a clothing store in Regent Street. Debbie's mother had just come from Bartica up the Essequibo River, out of the "Bush," to seek out the wider world. They met when she was taken on as a salesgirl in the Hirwani store on Regent Street in the early 1960s. It was a time when the stores of the Indian merchants on Regent and Water Streets were being torched and looted by Blacks, in what degenerated into something close to a racial civil war. The East Indian Marxist populist Dr Cheddi Jagan, the first premier of British Guiana, was serving his third term. Even when the Governor called in the British army and the police, they did little to stop the looting and burning of the stores of the Indian merchants—often in broad daylight. Once more the Hirwani family, like many others in the face of the violence and instability they had run away from in the partition of

27

India, packed up and moved first to California then to Montreal. Did the spectre and uncertainty of a Quebec partition prompt the move to Toronto? The cycles of history!

Looking at him looking at the pictures, all the prejudice the Indians who were born in Guyana had against the Indian merchants who were born in India and who owned most of the large stores and businesses in Georgetown, came back. Perhaps it was this resentment too which fuelled the looting of the Indian stores by the Guyanese of African ancestry—a violence which though I could not excuse, I was beginning to understand. These Indian Indians did not mix with other Indians, were mean, underpaid their workers and did not permit trade unions among their employees whom they treated like personal servants. They acted as though they were superior to all the Indians born in the then British colony. To the rural Indians, these Indians from India were after all born in sacred "Bharat Desh" and were so handsome, like the Indian film stars, and dressed so well and were so fair!

These "Indians" were Sindhis who had the *reputation* throughout India of being very unscrupulous businessmen, according to our Hindi professor who was from UP in India. This was a revelation, as was the fact that the group of Sindhis in our class who grew up in Guyana did not know much Hindi, at least not as much as most of us who were born in Guyana.

"I took this out in a photo studio on Regent Street—run by the Mohammed brothers I think," he said, holding the picture of himself.

"The Acme Photo Studio now. A complex and huge operation—perhaps the largest photography establishment in the country, occupies almost an entire block." I volunteered.

"So Jagan might finally get back into power." He said suddenly with an edge to his voice. "He brought the wrath of the US and the British down on the Indians, and during that time the impression of American officials was that once you were Indian and were in anyway connected to British Guiana, you were communist—he and his Marxism did."

His knowledge of the possibility of Jagan's return to office surprised me. I spoke passionately against British and American interference in the region's politics, and he took that to be a defence of Jagan. I let it go at that.

"May I keep these for a while?" He indicated the photographs.

"Yes." I was angry with myself for being intimidated and unsettled by him. He was playing with me, testing my control.

"And could you not tell her you met me—at least not yet—let me think about this for a while. I will call you as soon as I have thought this through."

I nodded and he rose and gave me his hand—it was firm and I detected a certain warmth. Outside, through the window behind him, the red sky, the sindhur sun, the glittering lake, the circling gulls, the boats of pleasure and leisure on the lake, the Saguenay line ship heading for the Redpath sugar terminal—most likely bearing Guyana's "Demerara sugar" for refining—all combined in a picture-postcard beauty. I turned and headed for the elevator, in my mind the Saguenay line ships of childhood sailing up along the coast at nights, lit like palaces, heading for the sugar loading terminals. We would run to our windows and verandahs for the spectacle of lights moving on water, wondering about the lands beyond. Later we lost that innocence. Those very ships became symbols of the colonising north. The buying of sugar and bauxite for next to nothing, repackaging, "refining" and selling the "finished, refined" products of sugar and bauxite back to the south for a hundred times the original price. Little wonder Jagan and almost all the politicians of his era in South America and the West Indies were "anticapitalists."

That first day!

That first day I saw her sitting on the other side of the desk I had come to feel my own, because I had not shared it with anybody for so long, two things registered instantly. She had neatly arranged my books on my side of the desk and even in profile she was beautiful. We were short staffed and had been expecting a replacement to teach Spanish since the previous term, but the replacement did not arrive and with the acute shortage of teachers—who were being recruited in the other West Indian countries, since many were leaving the country in the mass exodus to flee the "Kabaka" dictatorship—we were beginning to think that we would have a long wait. School had just reopened after the August holidays and during the general assembly in the main building that Monday, the principal had announced that the Ministry of Education would be sending a replacement—he did not elaborate and I was preoccupied with the English teachers' symposium which I would be attending the following two days. We had been looking at the effects of the Caribbean Examination Council English and Literature examinations, which had replaced the London GCE Examinations. The CXC, as the Caribbean examinations were known, were more comprehensive; the Caribbean content was greater. We were apprehensive that many of the older teachers would have difficulty relating to and teaching West Indian Literature, brought up in a time when the notion that English literature was the preserve of the English and American writers was generally accepted and propagated by the education system.

When I entered the small staff room and approached the desk she looked up and smiled. Her round, brown eyes set my heart going like the older of the two Massey-Ferguson tractors we had back home on the Corentyne Coast.

"Morning," I ventured.

"Good Morning," she answered. The vigour in her voice was startling.

"Our new Spanish Teacher?" I asked.

"Yes," she said as if throwing a challenge. I believe we both fell in love then. There was that awkward silence that always follows when two people are greatly attracted to each other, when they recognize this attraction and are unsure how to move on from there without disturbing what's there, without spoiling that unspeakable fullness and intoxication of experience.

"Welcome to South City. I did not expect someone as young and as pretty as you. You're as beautiful as Nargis—no, much more beautiful." I had assumed that she was Indian and that she knew that Nargis was one of the most beautiful Indian film stars. Stopping off in Greece, en route to India, even Naipaul had noted the large billboards with Nargis. One of Nargis's greatest films—one of the few very good films I had seen—*Mother India*—was being screened at the Liberty Cinema. There was a question on her face which I only understood later.

"Sorry. I'm Gopal Singh and I teach English and literature." There was a frown on her face and she turned to Kumar Nauth who was sitting at his desk and smiling. The others in our small staff room were also smiling.

"They told me it was best I share your desk. You were old, nearing retirement so you would leave soon anyway—and I would have nothing to fear from you . . ." I suspected this was the work of Kumar, who enjoyed his new position as the supervisor of our branch of South City High. The main building was a block and a half away. Separated from the main branch by houses, shops and several streets we enjoyed our autonomy. Kumar's was a quaint humour, but his good-natured quirks were condescending, as were his studied efforts at disguising the importance he attached to his supervisorship, his way of saying, "See I'm still one of you." The correct title was Branch Principal but he was sometimes referred to as the Hardy Branch Supervisor, as the branch was situated at the corners of Hardy and Savage streets.

"Oh, I'm Debbie Veira." She said as I sat down opposite her.

"You look very Indian," I said, suddenly conscious of the comparison to Nargis and feeling foolish.

"The only Indian I have is Amer-indian," and she laughed, barely opening her small, almost circular mouth. Her teeth were narrow, like the teeth of mice, but clean, unstained and white and her lips were full and a rich, natural pink."And a very small part at that. My mother's Arawak, Scottish and Portuguese, and my father very Portuguese," she said, with emphasis on *Portuguese*. Her face was a face I had seen in various plates of Hindu temple sculpture and Hindu iconography in various art books at the library. It was a time when I was reentering

my Hindu world intellectually. I had come from the Corentyne Coast
to go to the university and was living in Alberttown with my brother
and his wife. Up until graduation I had lost my teenage enthusiasm for
Hinduism but with graduation, it pulled me again. The five years of
constant criticism, subtle and unsubtle, the assault by the "Kabaka"
government on Indian life and customs—especially Hindu life—having built up pressure in me like steam in a pressure cooker, I let out in
research, in the search of that Hinduness which I discovered many
scholars felt to be one of the great world philosophies.

So when I saw Debbie that first time, after having looked at and
studied all that Indian art, I was positive I was looking at features of
the exquisite north Indian sculptures. Later she said that her father,
Anthony Veira, was born in Brazil and had come to Guyana alone as
a teenager. He had never gone back even though he had become an
important director in one of the largest shipping companies. He no
longer had relatives there, she said in his defence, but she felt tied to
Brazil and to a lesser extent Portugal—these were her "mother countries": Brazil first then Portugal, so she was learning Brazilian Portuguese at the Brazilian cultural centre. As the weeks progressed our
attraction grew stronger, and I believed that it was evident to all those
around us that we were in love. When we had non-teaching periods at
the same time, we would sit at our desk and grade exercises, plan our
work—often we looked out the little window near us in the mornings
when the wind blasted the huge, centuries-old silk-cotton trees so their
leaves shouted glories to faceless gods and commanded us to listen.
There was magic in the wind and those trees. Most of the times my
mind was with her, and I marvelled at her ability to concentrate on her
work while my thoughts were engrossed with her. She said later she
was afraid to look too strongly at me because she feared that I would
see what was happening to her, and she was afraid of our differences.

But I found this difference attractive—what were these Christians
like? These Portuguese who were the bulwarks of the Roman Catholic
church in our country.

One morning she said, "I heard part of your lesson yesterday—you speak very eloquently of the church next door."

"The architecture of that old Anglican church is more eloquent than I could ever be—it's a pity they're letting it go to pieces. Parts of the steeple are falling off—this government will see the ruin of this country . . ."

"Don't blame the government in this instance—it's the people who run the church . . ." she said, adding, "we have many more churches than the Anglicans but we maintain them . . ."

"Sure—because many of the wealthy business people are Portuguese who have helped to bring this government to power! People who continue to support this, this government—you get concessions of all sorts . . ."

It had come out with a bitterness I had not intended.

"And what about Father Darke and the *Catholic Standard*?" She asked quietly.

"Father Darke was a man I respect, and he will be remembered whenever democracy, for which he was murdered, returns to this country . . . but . . ." The recollection was still painful. I was outside the courthouse that morning when he was murdered in broad daylight with hundreds of people around. The photographs in the next issue of *The Caribbean Contact,* published in Barbados, showed a "Black Jew" of the "House of Hebrews"—a group led by a black American fugitive who claimed the real Hebrews were blacks, as was Christ—running towards Father Darke with a bayonet, and then in the act of stabbing him to death. The name of the photographer was never published. He too would have been murdered.

"But—" she persisted quietly.

"But Darke was not Guyanese or Portuguese. He was an Irish priest working as a photographer for the *Catholic Standard*. And the editor of the *Catholic Standard* is neither Guyanese nor Portuguese. He's Irish too." The publication of the Catholic Church was one of the few weeklies that consistently exposed the corruption and racism of the government.

"And don't forget that the Portuguese party, the UF, formed a coalition with Burnham to ensure that the PPP and Jagan stayed out of power," I said, launching into a diatribe.

"It's lunchtime," she smiled, making all the politics seem unimportant. I felt foolish.

"Are you going home?" I asked.

"No—its hot today and I've walked with a little snack. Where do you have lunch?" She asked.

"Here if it's raining—but if it is sunny, like now, I go out under that tamarind tree. It's breezy and away from the cricket pitch and students running about and making noise. Let's go, you'll like it . . ."

As soon as we sat in the shade of the tree she observed, "there are students under all the trees around the compound—there are no students under this one. Lots of shade here?"

"It is believed that this tree is haunted," I said. It had taken me a lot of enquiring to learn that. The groundsman of twenty years had told me that a boy who was about to urinate under the tree was slapped and left unconscious—the slap, by an unseen force, was witnessed by other students from the school window. This had happened three years before I joined the staff. There were other smaller incidents over the years, and it seemed that any act of uncleanliness or of littering the area around this tree precipitated some punitive reaction from the unseen force—the "spirit" which haunted the tree.

"Why do you come here then?" She asked, looking around.

"Because I have the tree all to myself without any interruptions, and because I do believe there are spirits here. There are spirits all around us everywhere we go. Some good, some bad. I believe if we do not disturb those spirits they don't disturb us. And sometimes even if we do disturb them they won't trouble us—not if our own spirit is strong. Are you afraid?"

"No."

"Good. Then I'll tell you that this entire playfield and the land on which the school rests—and the neighbouring playfield and that huge space in front of the Anglican church next door, was once a huge cemetery. The spirits which are around are good ones. I get an extraordinary sense of peace when I come here, and somehow I feel the peace and quiet I get when I come here help me to see down, down into myself —down into time. Sometimes I see this place as it was when the Dutch first arrived here. I see them searching, seeking the fertile land and revelling in its fertility. I see the French and British after them interested in bringing order, dams, roads . . . so they could better extract and enjoy the riches of the soil and the sweat of their labourers, to build and enrich Europe. And then planting trees along roadways, often foreign trees to recreate and remind them of their Europe—there is so much here—so much . . ."

The formality with which she introduced me to her father was like an introduction from a nineteenth-century novel. I had already met her mother at a function at the Brazilian Cultural Centre when Debbie, who went to learn Portuguese there, was one of a group of students performing a folk song in Portuguese as part of a show highlighting Brazilian culture. She introduced me to her mother with just, "My mother," and "Mommy, Gopal." She was taller than her mother, and slimmer, and her hair was long and black while her mother's was sandy, cut short and curled inward.

I had taken her home on several occasions but had always avoided her father, though I had seen him on their verandah once with some friends or relatives. When I entered the house her father was reading the newspaper. He took off his spectacles, put them on the newspaper and rose. He was about five feet ten inches tall and stockily built, with a slightly protruding belly and strands of grey in his wavy black hair.

"Gopal, meet my father Mr Anthony Santos Herrera Veira." The length of the name staggered me. It was as though she was announcing the arrival of a great personage rather than introducing her father to me. I knew she had great respect for her father—she spoke Portuguese with him, she used his dictionaries which he had possessed for many years, and she was proud that he was born in Brazil. She spoke of Bahia, Para', Parana', with a quaint roll of her tongue that I liked to listen to, and of the major cities Manaus, Boa Vista, Rio, Sao Paulo which I had read or heard of in the news from time to time but which somehow suddenly seemd nearer and more real. She was always telling me she wanted to visit Brazil (and Portugal) and in a way I understood, it was how I felt about India, about wanting to find what remained of my relatives there and to travel the country. But her introduction staggered me. It was an awkward meeting with her father and we spoke of little trivial things until she returned and led me out onto the verandah.

Soon I caught some of her fever about Brazil and to a lesser extent Portugal. If I read something interesting or good about any of the two countries I would tell it to her and she glowed. And I learnt about Brazil and Portugal from her. I started to read as much as I could about both countries so when she spoke about either I knew something—the history of Portuguese colonialism in India!

One day while we were sitting on a bench in the National Park she said suddenly, "Gopal—I've never met your parents, not even your brother and his wife with whom you live. I would like to meet them." I had been dreading this for a long time and I had hoped, in a way, that by being involved and immersed in her world, I could avoid all of this.

"When I introduce you to my family, especially my parents, it means I plan to marry you. And I believe that any girl I take home, my parents would expect me to get married to. I mean no criticism but for us a boyfriend or girlfriend going home is serious business. I couldn't take you home without discussing it first with my parents, and once I took you home, my parents would start thinking of a time and day for the wedding . . ."

"Do they know about me?" She asked.

"My brother and sister-in-law know—they saw you when we were on the seawall last week . . ."

"And you didn't introduce them, even point them out to me . . .?" There was smothered anger in her voice. "Is this just a fling for you then?" She was angry and this was a rare thing for her. I didn't respond but there was no avoiding a quarrel.

"No. But before we think seriously of marriage we have got to think further, of children. How are we going to bring them up? As

Hindus, as Roman Catholics, as neither? How are we going to live our lives—separately? You Christian and I Hindu? You to your Mass, I to Mandir. And the question of food? I don't eat beef . . ."

"Okay—how would you see a marriage? What would you compromise, give up?" She asked.

"Nothing maybe —I don't know," I said.

"Nothing! Isn't that unfair? Why don't men ever change?" Her eyes got rounder.

"Maybe it is unfair, but that is not the point for me. Where I come from in the country, every time a Hindu man marries a Moslem woman—they convert him, change his name. Every time a Hindu man marries a Christian woman, they convert him and all the children are Christians. Is that fair? Look at your Portuguese next door in Brazil— Christianized the largest land mass on the South American continent. Did they convert to the religions of the Amerindians, the speech of the Amerindians? No, they converted the Amerindians or exterminated them! And your Portuguese in Africa, Angola, in India, in Goa, in China, Macau . . ."

"Are you going to crucify me for that?"

"No, but I am not going to be crucified as they were. Listen, how many months have we been going out? I know almost everything you know, maybe more about your world. I have gone to Mass with you. What do you know about my world? How many times have you ever enquired about my world? And if ever we were to get married and have children and we brought them up as Hindus—they would still know as much, maybe more about Christianity . . . Like me, I am Hindu but when I went to school, to University everything was explained in relation to the Christian world, the European world. All the references in the literature I did were Judeo-Christian, Roman, Greek and we had to go and research the references especially in the poetry to 'understand'! I know more about Christianity than most of the people who walk around trying to convert me, who come in my yard seeing a Jhandi flag and tell me I worship idols—that Christ is the only way to god. Thank heavens for the CXC—though that too is still basically Judeo-Christian, but at least we teach Naipaul; and you know half the jokers who teach Naipaul and comment on Naipaul's *House for Mr Biswas* don't even know who was Hanuman—don't know the importance of *Hanuman katha* among the Hindus of Trinidad and Guyana up to today, or the significance of Tulsi to Hindus. Teach Naipaul . . .!"

Everything that had no direct bearing to her was coming out.

"Yes but what about me—and my convictions too. If we did all you wanted then would you be any better than the people you criticize?"

"No. I would not," I answered and after a long pause I added, "that's why perhaps the others may be right, marriages across racial, cultural and religious lines can't work . . ."

"And why not? And what about us?" She asked taking my hand, "what about love? The power and purity of love? You once said love was casteless, colourless, genderless, you remember—yoga?"

"Yes I remember. But duty, *Dharma—one has to do what one has to do*—overrides everything, even personal feelings . . ."

"So are you saying our relationship is over?"

"No. We can still continue as we have been all this time . . ."

"But no marriage? And for how long?"

"I don't know. What I do know is that hurrying will not get us anywhere—I might change or you might, we both might . . ." The thought of a separation had sobered us. We had never contemplated such a possibility before. Did she assume I would change, become a Catholic, especially as I had accompanied her around to Mass, to fairs and her cultural shows? And did I not feel that when the time came, she would adapt to my Hinduism and so I saw no need to peddle it?

We made love that night with a passion as we never had before and when I took her home on my motorcycle she squeezed me very tightly from behind, and I think she must have cried a little in the dark, behind me. School closed for three weeks, for the Christmas and New Year holidays and I went home to the Corentyne Coast. She had wanted me to spend Christmas with her but my parents were doing a Jhandi because my eldest sister was coming from Canada during the holidays.

My sister had married and gone to Canada almost fifteen years before and this was her first trip back. There was a lot of work to do and a lot of preparation. Her husband, also from our village, was coming too.

But my sister and her husband and their sponsoring of us took second place to my reentry into a world I thought I had left behind for good. Going around with my brother-in-law along the coast was a long series of drinking bouts, especially in that last week leading up to New Year. The hospitality and warmth we were shown was something I missed in Georgetown. People opened their hearts and houses to us. And there was the famous No. 63 beach in the neighbouring village: the "bumper-ball" cricket on the sand in the rain, the food cooking on the sand under the coconut trees while we played cricket, and drank white rum with coconut water, and bathed in the sea. We sang Sundar-Popo and Indian filmi songs and danced on the sand; we danced and sang in homes of friends we visited, in the rum shops we frequented along the coast.

Then there was talk between my mother and my sister of "fixing" me up with some girl from Crabwood Creek. My sister and my mother had just returned from a trip to the area to meet some of my sister's friends. But Ravi, my brother-in-law, who had heard of Debbie in one of our drinking sprees (I must have been drunk and full of self-pity and guilt, and while the "punch-box" was playing Mukesh's famous, *"Tu akaylaa saath, tu akaylaa hai . . .,"* 'Alone with you, you are alone . . . , I told him and the others something of Debbie—I don't remember exactly what) came to my aid. Marriage would affect my sponsorship! The Friday before school reopened, the day my sister and Ravi returned to Canada, we came back to Georgetown to my brother's place on Fourth Street from the airport. My parents would be staying for the weekend before they travelled back to the Corentyne Coast.

We were on the verandah when my father asked suddenly, "So yuh like dhis Debbie gyaal?" It caught me off guard and it was some time before I could respond. I looked around unconsciously, glad my mother was inside with Basdeo's wife.

"Yeh Pa, but we jus teach a' school together, yuh know . . . an' if it could wuk then a'think about it. Mih na reddy yet Pa," I said trying to sound as casual as possible.

"Yuh know yuh mumma na like dhis fooling'round . . ."

"Tru' mih na like dhis ting Gopal . . ." My mother had come on to the verandah quietly, "If yuh like wan a'nather get married. Na fool nobady. Remember yuh gat sista too." I knew what would follow. "Why na bring dhe gyaal leh we see she?"

"Ma —na anything serious, we just teach together," I repeated.

"Neva mind."

"Yes Gopal, why yuh hiding this girl," Basdeo said, "why not bring her tomorrow. I'm anxious to see her myself." He laughed.

The next morning Basdeo gave me his car: the "old people" might be unfavourably impressed if they saw her on my motorcycle with her arms around me, as he had seen us a few times! I didn't phone her and she was surprised to see me at such an early hour—it was only 9 a.m. She had on a pink floral frock that fitted her well. I looked into her round brown eyes and I wanted to kiss her.

She pushed in the door and started to say, "Oh how I missed—" And I quickly kissed her.

"Me too," I said, 'You look so lovely. Let's go for a drive—"

"Now! Jenny and I are going to the market to buy fish an' greens—"

"Jenny can go by herself—she'll understand. Tell your mother and let's go."

"Okay—let me change."

"No. This is fine . . ." I was afraid she would put on one of her tight fitting trousers. I wanted my parents to like her—and my mother would note everything. I was worried about their reaction, especially when they found out that she was not Hindu, or even Indian.

"My brother's car I said."

"Really!" She said getting in.

"Oh, I missed you," she said as we moved off, squeezing my leg, "I've something very important to tell you." There was silence as I concentrated on the road and the Saturday morning traffic.

"I want to learn about Hinduism, to be Hindu—will you help me?"

I was surprised and wanted to look at her face.

"If you want me to, I can teach you what I know of Hinduism . . ."

"I want to. I want to see your face, your eyes, to tell you this, this . . ." her voice trailed off and when I glanced quickly at her there was a certain sadness.

"Not now—when I'm in this traffic . . ." I responded and from the corner of my eyes I saw her nodding in agreement. They were on the verandah as I drove unto the bridge. And suddenly it dawned on her.

"Where are we going?"

"To meet my brother and his wife and my parents—they want to see you . . ."

"Gopal—why didn't tell me. This is so sudden . . . I'm nervous." She looked at her clothes.

"Don't worry, you look fine—and there's my sister-in-law, she's alright, she'll help you—she went through this too . . . Let's go, they are waiting." I squeezed her fingers. From the moment we went into the verandah I felt they liked her, they were taken by her as much as I was when I first saw her.

"Come," my mother said, taking her hand, "gad bless yuh gyaal." And she said it with such simplicity and feeling that there was a hush for a few seconds after. We all knew that there was more than a simple blessing in the short statement. In it my mother had welcomed her into our family, accepted her as a daughter-in-law in a way no wedding ceremony, or certificate of marriage could. Even Debbie, not too familiar with our ways, felt that. I felt such gratitude for my mother and her blessing. And my mother sat her down beside her and looked at me and smiled.

Basdeo said laughingly, "I can understand now why Gopal hardly at home for the last couple months now." The remark seemed to add some lightness and I felt happy, so that what happened next surprised me.

"Yuh Hindu na," my mother half asked, half stated in her matter-of-fact way. My heart skipped a few beats when I saw Debbie nod in agreement. I was amazed at her nod, and more amazed when she looked at me and I saw tears start rolling down her cheeks. Meena, my sister-in-law got up quickly and went across to her and put her arm round her and with my mother they went into the house. My father shook his head and Basdeo said, "Very beautiful." And we waited in silence. When they came out back after about twenty minutes my mother said, "Gopal yuh bad."

"Gopal why you didn't tell her you were bringing her here. You wouldn't like something like that to happen so suddenly to you, would you?" Meena added

"I'm sorry, I only wanted to surprise her." And turning to her I said, "I'm sorry . . ." And she smiled and said nothing and they went into the house again. They liked her very much and said that when next Basdeo and Meena were going to the Corentyne Coast she could visit—if she wanted to. Debbie was delighted. She had never been to Berbice before, she had never even set eyes on the Berbice river.

On Monday it rained, so we could not go under the tamarind tree for lunch. And she reminded me that she had something important to tell me—the staff room was not private and so after school we went to the Botanical gardens under the huge "Cheese-and-bread" tree near the manatee pond, which was one of our favourite spots. The fierce afternoon sun had dried the higher land around the root of the tree. I felt this important thing she wanted to tell me was that she was pregnant. There were light-dark lines under her eyes and that worried look.

"So what's so important you cancelled your Portuguese class?"

"I don't feel like doing Portuguese anymore . . ." she said. I was shocked. It was one of the more important things in her life.

"Why?"

"That's just it—I just learnt my father's not my real father. My mother gave birth to me before she met my father, I mean my present father. My real father was Indian. He came from India and had a store in Regent Street and my mother worked for him and just after the riots when my mother got me, he went to Canada. I was about a year. He used to support us, but his parents would not agree to his marrying my mother. In that hard, lonely time my mother met my father, my present father, who married her and agreed to give me his name. My real father still used to write and send money but my present father stopped that and my mother lost touch with him. He's married and has children too."

What could I say? It tumbled out of her and she was confused and uncertain. This was a surprise. I had not been wrong after all in thinking her "Indian" when I first saw her. I remembered, in those moments we looked at each other, her former cockiness and pride in her Portugueseness. She lowered her eyes. I believed that she must have been conscious of all those things too. There was nothing I could say, to tell her I felt her hurt and confusion and I didn't want to say anything that might inadvertently hurt her further. I put my arm round her shoulder and she put her arms around me, her face in my chest. She was sobbing. My mother, on meeting her, had assumed too she was Indian. Debbie had started to cry then because my mother's remark brought her face to face again with this. During the Christmas holidays her mother had felt the time had come to tell her about her real father—and the knowledge shamed her. The man whom she believed to be her own father had always treated her as his favourite. And she had, over the years, thrown such tantrums, which he had always excused because she was his favourite daughter. She was his only daughter who showed any interest in his world, his Portuguese Brazilian Catholic world—and now she had stopped her Portuguese classes. How could she face her teachers at the Centre? All the pride and interest in Portuguese and Brazilian, and Brazil! And there was the Indian world she had shunned only to learn it was a greater part of herself. And whom could she discuss it with but me, with whom she had shared her pride in her Portugueseness!

Later, when it was easier for her to talk about it, I said, "But you are still Portuguese—your mother . . ."

"A very small part," she said, not without some humour in her eyes.

"You can continue your Portuguese . . ."

"No. I don't think I could ever continue Portuguese—it could never

43

be the same, I did it because of what I thought . . ."

"Because your 'father' wanted one of his children to do it? The fact that he is not your father is perhaps more reason why you should continue it? This man who knew all along you were not his daughter and yet—you are his daughter and he your father."

"That makes sense but it's not so simple Gopal . . ."

"Yes, we know that don't we, emotions make a mockery of reason . . ." I teased.

"I'd like to meet him . . ." she said, speaking of her real father.

"You should see *Kabhie kabhie,*" I told her, mentioning the Indian film. "There is some similarity in it to our situation." I believe this comment of mine led to her romance with Indian films.

"And all these years I almost despised Indians, didn't know I was Indian . . ."

The elevator opens and two women exit first: the lobby bathed in the reflected sunlight and their bronzed legs, gym-fit figures, the blonde hair of one, the bleached-blonde hair of the other . . . Even the blonde has borrowed the tandoori brownness. The bleach-blonde turns and smiles! Large brown eyes in a brown face! An Indian trying to "fit in," to run away from her "Indianness"?

Yehudi Menuhin, commenting on the music of Pandit Ravi Shankar, once said that listening to the music of Ravi Shankar's genius, one not only enters the Indian world, one becomes Indian—the universal primal soul transcending all caste and class and differences.

Debbie had finally said to me: "So I am Indian after all!"

And I had asked, more of myself, "And who, and what is Indian?" We had laughed; a laughter now echoing down this hole in this earth, at this Toronto subway stop!

Is There No Laughter in Snow?

It was a hot, sticky afternoon in December and nobody felt like working. Strains of Christmas carols, preparations for the holidays, that nostalgic sweet-sad remembrance of childhoods and anticipation of futures, all combined and contributed to that infectious not-feeling-like-working atmosphere that Christmas always brings. Baxter mentioned something about the diploma in public administration he was doing at the University.

And I said, not without some sarcasm, "That will put you in line for a directorship. The comptroller is due to retire next year and so is Kissoon." Kissoon was one of three assistant comptrollers of the Customs and Excise Department. I added, "Williams and Meredith, according to the grapevine, are going to leave the department for greener pastures." Williams and Meredith, who were contemplating doing their doctoral dissertations, were the other two assistant comptrollers. They were of African ancestry and had been promoted ahead of all the officers in line for their positions. Almost all of the officers they superseded were Indians—the older officers of the department.

"I should be retiring with Dannet too, but I ain't staying so long." Everyone turned to Dutt, surprised. Dutt looked forty-one or two. There was a silence and Dutt continued, "Early next year I should be getting through to Region Eleven." There was a snicker. The country was divided into ten administrative regions. North America was jokingly referred to as Region Eleven.

There was silence again until Baxter broke it. "Man Dutt, how lang you in this wuk?"

"*'Wuk*, you call *this* wuk . . . Anyway yuh right is wuk now . . ." The bitterness in Dutt's voice was startling. This was unusual for Dutt. Slowly he shook his head. "When I joined this department, a customs officer was like a king. If yuh going aboard a ship and a stevedore see some grease on the gangway he hustle to wipe it away—now . . ." Dutt paused and shook his head sideways. His voice rang with contempt. "Now, when dhem stevedore see a officer coming dhe hustling fuh turn dhe back from he, hustling fu hide what dhe gat because the officer coming fuh he share!" There was laughter at this exaggeration.

"Dutt how lang yu in dis department?" Baxter asked again.

"Before any one-a-you in hey born. I working here thirty-two years now!"

Baxter, the oldest of us, was only thirty one.

"You joined before the comptroller?" I asked.

"Yes, two month before. That man ruin this department! Imagine police telling Customs what to do! Ridiculous! I could write a book about how that man and this government bugger up this department—a bestseller! When I joined was a different time, a different world!" I leaned back into my chair as his bitterness seeped into me. We were sitting in a rough circle. Dutt's head was framed by the brilliant blue sky in the north, behind and over his head. There were no clouds, no birds in the sky. At twenty-nine, I had almost the same rank as Dutt but we all knew, those of us who were much younger and almost the same rank as Dutt and the officers of his generation, that our knowledge of customs and excise procedures was nowhere close to that of Dutt's. Perhaps our knowledge of customs law was, but excise law and practice . . . ? Dutt was one of the few excise authorities in the country and his expertise in distilleries and breweries was so well known that he had received several very lucrative offers from the private sector. Perhaps Dutt liked the feel of authority, as did we, those of us who were younger and who liked it so much that we permitted ourselves to be used in the system to the detriment of Dutt and the older officers. "But it was beautiful and enjoyable too." Dutt was his usual jovial self again. "Sometimes," he continued, "when we had nothing much to do we would tell jokes. A night, a big North American or British ship was discharging—I think was the *Booker Viking*. Anyway was me and Griffith working. All yuh ain't gun know Griffith. He in England now. All yuh ever hear the story of King Arthur and the knights of the Round Table?" He didn't pause. "Well, according to Griffith, King Arthur had to go on some mission alone and he know dhem bhai, the knights, gun want seduce dhe Queen, so he put a chastity belt on she. But this belt was no ordinary belt. Through the pee-hole had two sharp blades that automatically cut off anything going through. Well, Sir Arthur set off. Fust thing when he come back, he call all he knights in he room and order dhem fuh drap dhem pants. Everyone-a-them except Sir Galahad had dhem prick cut off. Sir Arthur get mad saying he ain't gat no loyal knights except Sir Galahad. He run up to Sir Galahad asking he what he want as reward for he loyalty. All Sir Galahad could say was 'Uu Uu Uu Uu.' " Dutt imitated a dumb man. There was laughter. "All dhem other knights try to use dhem prick, but Sir Galahad try to use he tongue instead—lose he tongue . . ." Dutt laughed and continued, "When Griffith telling me this thing I jus bus out one big laugh when bam! Blackout! Now this was about ten o' clock in the night and dhem stevedores down in the hatch. You could imagine what happen! One big commotion and noise start in the hatch. All we hear was paper ripping up and cardboard tearing! Bam! In about thirty seconds light come on back. When we look down the hatch more confusion. All dhem stevedores spitting out all they had in dhe mouth and shouting at one another. 'You eat um too, you eat um too?' And more confusion. When the sling come out the hold, Griffith and me decide to check the goods on the sling— guess what? Dhem stevedores eat Kerr's Dog Biscuits!—Sombady just see *Biscuit* on the packing!"

Before we could finish laughing Dutt went on, "Another time I was working at Timehri Airport. In them days Atkinson Airbase. I was collecting duty and there was a lang line of incoming passengers to pay duty. After about half hour, a beautiful Indian girl approached the counter. So I took her assessment slip and as I start write up the receipt, I said, 'Madam what's your name?'

" 'Jean,' she said smiling.

" 'Your whole name, Madam,' I asked. She continued smiling, probably thinking I was getting fresh—I was young then. I was getting impatient. 'Madam what's your whole name?' I repeated. She looked around shyly and smiled. I get really mad then and asked harshly in creolese, 'Woman what yuh whole name? If yuh want dhis receipt write, yuh better answer.' She looked around again and said tartly, 'Mih hole name pussy!' "

We were laughing again, and again before we could finish he went on.

Looking directly at me he asked, "Anand, you remember when I was in charge of Long-room and you were doing shipping bills?"

I nodded. Long-room was the name by which the collections section was known. All documentary assessment and checking of customs and excise duties were done there. In the fifties, before independence, when there was a lot of international trade, the British officers who were in charge of the department had all the officers in this section in one long, open room for easier surveillance. The name stuck.

"You were in the hospital for a month when you had your accident. At the same time, I think it was Lyson Knitwear lost their customs broker. The new chap, a *country-bai,* brought a shipping bill for a consignment of panties to the US. The moment I looked at the tariff heading number I know it wrong. Articles of clothing is usually Chapter 64. He had Chapter 85—articles of steel. So I sent for him and pointed out that the heading was wrong, the duty wrong. He started to argue. So to prove the point I gave him the tariff and told him to find the tariff heading he used. When we found his heading, 85.06, the description we found was MAN HOLE COVERS—articles of steel!"

There was laughter and then the phone rang. I was required in the registry.

An hour later when I returned, Dutt and everyone else were diligently at work. I sat down at my desk but could not concentrate on the investigation I was assigned. There was that blue sky outside and the heat and moisture under my arms—we had just moved into the new Customs and Excise Building and the airconditioner which had been freezing us in the morning was being rechecked—and there was pain, Dutt's pain and bitterness gnawing at my consciousness. Dutt's pain and bitterness were also those of the East Indians since independence from the British, when they became the victims of a perverse discrimination. . . . The more I worked with Dutt, the more I realized that he hid his frustration in laughter.

I remembered another of Dutt's anecdotes—somebody else's joke no doubt. According to Dutt he had arrived home at about two a.m. after a hard night at the airport. He had just fallen asleep when there was loud knocking on his door. His wife went to check. Their neighbour's daughter was suffering from terrible belly pain. He was the only person in the village with a car and the doctor was six miles away. Could he take them to the doctor? According to Dutt he was so sleepy and angry he would have refused but for his wife. At the doctor's office, the doctor spent some time examining the daughter then came out into the outer office where Dutt and the parents were waiting. The doctor was bombarded with questions,

"Dac wha wrang? Dac wa wrang?"

"Your daughter is pregnant," he said.

"Impassable," the mother.

"Impassable," the father.

"Dhat gyal don't see no bai. Dhat gyal na lef house fu go no way. Dhat impassable!" from both mother and father. "Dac yuh sure, Dac yuh certain . . . ?" The doctor went to his eastern window and began scanning the sky. After about five minutes the mother asked, "Dacta wha wrang?"

"Wrong! I'm looking for the star in the eastern sky! The last time something like this happened there was a big bright star in the eastern sky. I don't want to miss it this time!" There had been the usual laughter when Dutt had told this tale, but I had missed Dutt's mockery of the virgin birth . . .

Sitting there, all the pieces suddenly started to fall in place. The King Arthur story—a reward to the dumb, a joke on men! Who ate dog biscuits? Who were the stevedores? Was it the racism? Even the officers of African ancestry laughed at Dutt's recycled stories. What was important? The laughter, the relief, the stories, or the telling?

"Man Anand, if I was a writer like you . . . .!" Dutt had exclaimed one day. "I could write a book on this department—a real rass book!" he said over and over, prefacing each session of his story-telling. Nobody could work then.

All Dutt had to show for a lifetime of labour was humour, smiles, laughter; but deep down, what was there? Dutt coped using his stories and humour. I thought I would use skill and hard work: I would be better than any officer who was my contemporary! My performance was justification for my promotions—but this only made it easier for them. Instead of putting their hands in the hat and coming up with any Indian name—"See we also promote young Indian officers . . ." my promotions could be justified. Soon, like Dutt there would be no place else to go. What would I do then when I bumped into that dark wall of racism and corruption? Suruj, a brilliant young officer was murdered because he had uncovered too much on the trail of corruption. His conscience could not allow him to let it go. Would mine? Others had all gone away, one by one. Region Eleven. And now Dutt was going, having awakened us to the mask of his smile. I stacked the documents neatly on my desk and then locked them away for another day. The river was too far. But it wasn't for Baxter who had requested a transfer to "where the action was."

A year later when Baxter heard that we were coming to audit the documents at his wharf, he had cooly walked up to the raging river and dumped out all the documents. Broad daylight, dozens of people on the wharf unloading a Dutch ship but none of the stevedores, nobody, would testify. Baxter had once worked in the Investigation section with us! Our unit arrived five minutes too late! And who would find documents in the mouth of the Demerara, flowing out to the Atlantic?

Capping his laughter Baxter said, "Skipper Dhe rats must-be eat them documents out. All a yu wuk at the waterfront aready! Yu know how dem rats big like cat!" Baxter winked at me when the others from our investigation unit went down to the river. He took the next flight to Miami.

How did Dutt embellish this one?

When Dinesh had left just before his "runnings" were discovered, Dutt had said, "Rass bai, all you hear about Dinesh? He working the outgoing flight at Timehri last night; finish checking out outgoing passengers; walk out to the tarmac, walk up the airplane door like he going to check the cargo hold. He-he! Next thing door closing and Dinesh on he way to New York! He dress shirt hanging in the Customs locker room near he lunch bag with all he ID! Dhem bai seh Dinesh food still hot—roti and dhaal and curry karilla smelling up the place like rass! And a note on he bag saying: BOYS ENJOY! SEE YOU IN NY!"

I too walked away, leaving the laughter, a whole life behind; all those stories they burdened me with telling dissolving like these wet flurries on the warm windowpane. Subzero temperatures from my winter cage. Not long ago we slid down that slope on the hill—a ten-car pile-up—holding our hearts in our hands. We joked afterwards: how romantic the white stuff! Yuh think there is no laughter in snow?

When Men Speak This Way

These are of those early mornings on the river. Heaven came to earth for one hour and hell reigned in the following seven—and this is of that time when men speak that way. And all this years ago. I had been a junior shipping clerk at the old Bookers Wharf. In those days it had just been renamed the Guyana National Shipping Corporation by the Burnham government, which, firmly entrenched on a "socialist" policy, had nationalised the British Bookers Holdings in the country—the entire sugar industry and the bauxite industry, formerly owned by Americans and the Canadian multinational ALCAN. Business with the metropolitan countries which supplied all the machinery, even the ships to export the products of these nationalised industries, needless to say, was greatly reduced and unless a boat was alongside and discharging cargo it would be rather quiet at seven AM, the hour we opened the warehouse for business with the public. Normally it remained quiet until about eight AM when the large importers or their agents started calling, enquiring about short-shipped goods, short-landed goods, damaged goods, broached goods . . . And there were lots of those—broached goods. It was an importer's nightmare and doubly ours—as representing the shippers we were legally responsible for the security of the goods. Legality and law were a joke, yet for "influential" and "connected" people the law could be invoked with a vengeance.

Often, goods transshipped from a European or North American vessel at some West Indian island port, especially Port-of-Spain in Trinidad and later from Parimaribo in neighbouring Surinam, which was suffering from all sorts of shortages because of the 1980 coup, created headaches for us. Goods passing through these ports often arrived broached once these were not sealed in twenty- and forty-foot containers, yet even the containers were no guarantee that cargo would not be broached, and the Guyanese stevedores got all the blame. It was not that the Guyanese stevedores were angels, but they were not always the culprits though they did more than their share, unobserved, in the hatches of ships, or while loading or unloading at nights, in the dark hours of the early morning. It was rare to catch them in the act, but when we caught them we on occasion pretended we did not see—the effort of reporting, the investigations by customs or police all very time-consuming, so that we felt it was not worth it. Perhaps we were as corrupt as the stevedores and did not realise it, taking a perverse pleasure in having a hold over them when we knew they knew we saw them stealing and did not report them, but it was more because it was an embarrassment to catch them in the act and equally embarrassing to be caught pilfering.

But we knew what they did—everybody knew what they did, even the security at the gate. The stevedores, popularly called the "thiefadores" wore huge baggy trousers which easily concealed stolen articles, strapped tightly to their legs, calves and thighs. They lived well with the security guards at the checkout gate, which meant that the security guards got a percentage of the takings. Greed and especially need, we saw during this era, were the stimulants for acts of the greatest creative originality in dissimulation. Stevedores, who were experts at handling the winches and strapping crates to pallets, knew exactly which pallets were not quite securely strapped; these were the ones they put down on the wharf just a shade more roughly so that they spilled their scarce, expensive items on the greenheart planks, and it took a touch of diabolic genius to make several spilled items disappear in a trice. All the wharfingers cursed "these black bitches," even the "black" wharfingers. Paid by the hour and in blocks of four hours— four PM to eight PM; eight PM to midnight—they stretched the work past midnight if only by an hour so as to get paid for the entire 4 hour block . . . sleepy and bleary-eyed we cursed them all silently at night.

And we cursed them again and again during the day, mainly between eight AM to three PM as importers or their agents hounded us for their goods, maligned us for their broached goods. But that one hour from seven AM to eight AM when it was so quiet and peaceful made it all bearable. There would be little activity on the wharf, not even from the small ships and trawlers, a few of which would always be docked alongside the wharf. It was not that the occupants of these smaller vessels were not up or had nothing to do, but many of them, involved in many shady transactions, found it easier and safer to function when the wharf was alive with activity and people and the security and customs were engaged. In that first hour, from our office almost at the top of the huge warehouse, overlooking the majestic Demerara River, we read the newspapers, exchanged ideas, meditated on the frailty of man, the multiplicity of the Creator reflected in the River, cursed the government for ruining our country, cursed our people for being so docile and for participating in this destruction of a country once the haven and paradise of the English-speaking West Indies, the prized possession of the western half of the British crown. More often, I would go to my desk overlooking the River and open my ledgers; a sign that I had work to do, was not to be unnecessarily interrupted; a sign that I wanted to be left alone—alone to stare out into a paradise that no economic ruin, no political and racial discrimination, no blatantly rigged elections could take away from me. I loved to look at the indistinct vegetation on the distant west bank which curved with the river and the flat land along the river bank, not unlike the finely pencilled marks women took pride decorating their heads with, having taken off their eyebrows. And it would strike me that women's eyebrow liners were a poor imitation. Trees which broke the general line of the distant vegetation did not have to try all manner of artifice to find acceptance to the eye. Every morning, once there was no mist or rain on the river, I looked for the two tall palm trees, indistinct but recognisable as palms, which stood over all the other trees like the two eyes of god closed over the *lila*, the play and sport of his creation, the two eyes of god which could open at any moment. It was as though I did not want to miss this opening with its laser gaze.

But if the palms were the eyes, the river was god himself, full, calm, soft as Shiva meditating on *Kailash*. Sometimes it was sugar-brown, rain-muddied, flowing out to the Atlantic with branches, twigs, the fruits of the land, little pieces of gleaned wisdom flowing into the accommodating deluge of the ocean. Sometimes, the quiet river lapping at the logs of the wharf before the tide turned, sounded like the discourse of Arjuna and Krishna in the face of the two imposing armies about to destroy themselves in the great nuclear battle of the *Mahabharata* and of the planet earth. Then, the river pounded itself and everything else with a ferocity that was simultaneously bitter and sweet, and it was as though Shiva had come down from Kailash with fire in his eyes, power, grace, poetry in his feet—the *Nataraja* dancing his eternal and unmatched dance of love, destruction and creation. Sometimes there would be rain on the river and the other bank, the West bank, would be hidden in the silver wall of water—even ships in midstream would be hidden in the embrace of the falling water—and I would think;

from water to water
from cloud to river
from sea to sky . . .

and I would feel the urge to write the most beautiful poems in the world, poems as beautiful as Tulsidas's and perhaps I did too when I scribbled lines of poems on unused "blue books," lines still lying around in old drawers and dusty old cabinets containing documents from other decades, other lives; lines lost in the limbo of time and place. Who knows, perhaps some other junior clerk will come upon them and wonder at the manner of man I was, just as I spent some of those quiet moments looking at old ledgers, wiping away the dust of ages, looking at the handwriting and notes of my predecessors trying to learn something about them, their traits, their souls, their times . . . One thing had gradually dawned on me—and this was that their poetry of numbers left no doubt that they were masters of their pages: spillages were accounted for down to the decimal, ledgers balanced—everything started with and ended with zero.

That particular morning, Singh had been talking about his past. He was from Better-Hope Village on the East Coast and had worked all his life on the waterfront, at the Guyana National Shipping Corporation—GNSC—wharf as it had then become with the advent of nationalisation, but he, like most of the older men, always called it "Booka wharf." He was nearing retirement and he was suddenly conscious that he had nothing to show for his labour and worse, nothing to expect on his retirement now that there was an "illegal and corrupt" ruling clique. A pension was not certain. The government could decide to "retrench" him just before retirement as they had recently done to thousands of other workers (mostly Indians)—thereby not having to pay them pensions. His accumulated savings over the years, which would once have made a difference, now meant nothing in face of the years of "galloping" inflation since independence—fifteen years of it with no end in sight. He was worried but tried to be philosophical about it, and passed it off in a bitter-sweet reminiscence of the "good old days" when people cared . . . The "white" men were strict, but they cared for people, they rewarded a job well done. I had heard it all before but I always listened because although the theme was the same, he occasionally remembered a different story to illustrate and support his point. I could never bring myself to tell him that perhaps the "white" man did care—more for his profits than anything else. That he knew, after years of ruling people, the human resource was the greatest resource, his greatest asset in his march to amass money. So he had to appear to care—I was tempted to cite him Napoleon and his handout of ribbons, worthless ribbons, to his soldiers but I could never bring myself to disillusion him further. And maybe he was right. Maybe the "white" men he dealt with did care, even if in a guilt-ridden, condescending way, as much as they were permitted by the monster of a system which had spawned them; but then I could not quite bring myself to believe that some of them, seeing the wretchedness perpetuated by a system they administered, would remain untouched by it.

I listened to Singh's reminiscences because of the different stories he told to illustrate his various philosophical views. His stories were for me a journey back into a time I felt so close to, and he told these stories with such attention to detail, such vividness that I used to think that Singh must have been in lives past one of those great sages who orally handed down the knowledge and text of the *Vedas* and the great stories of the *Panchatantra* in Sanskrit without missing a *shloka,* a word, a pause. When the others were telling stories of the old days and there was any dispute about any detail they all turned to Singh for the correct version—and his version was accepted without question.

There had been a sudden silence that morning and we both looked out onto the quiet river, the crystal-clear morning, the billowy white clouds, the clean blue sky, the neatly etched waving outline of trees on the west bank—shades of green—and suddenly I spoke as I remembered from my past.

"Sometimes it was like this . . . "

"What?"

"The mornings at South City, when all was quiet . . . "

"Yes, yuh teach dhere . . . " he said looking out with me unto the morning river. Then quietly he got up.

"See you later," he said almost inaudibly.

"Yeph," I answered, knowing that he realised that I wanted to be left alone with the memories that were dearest to me and which I had not been willing to let go of yet. But I went back, hearing the kiskadees and blue sakies in the tamarind tree, the huge silk-cottons, the wrens in the crumpling steeple of the magnificent, century-old Anglican church nearby. During free periods, I would go downstairs alone and enjoy that paradise. The wind pattered on the leaves of the trees nearby and the coconut branches like rain in the distance, like the turning tide. That morning it all came back but stuck in my throat and I wasn't ready to talk about it, not yet, I thought, I haven't reached *that* stage. I turned to the newspaper to run away from it and started flipping through the pages. When I saw the announcement it shocked me. It said simply that Dr Philip Shiv Kumar had died quietly in his sleep in New York and had been cremated as was his desire. This numbed me for a while. Life and death were so simple—a few printed words on paper and that was it!

I remembered then, all those times I had gone to him—when I was sick and when I wasn't so sick but wanted leave—a little rest. Abdominal pain, back pain—he would quote the medical terms which I never remembered—and would ask of me, of himself, of the world, somewhat rhetorically; who could dispute that—nobody!

"Like the time I was doing exams in Glasgow and they were questioning me . . . " he would begin. If there was nobody else, he would sit and talk. He was such a smooth and rivetting talker and I liked to listen to him—the eloquence and poetry in his speech in a standard English that was natural and familiar, and from which he would slip into a phrase of Hindi-English. Somehow he always seemed to be talking about his years in medical school in Scotland; at least this was where he always began, it was his frame story from which he would wander off to tell of an incident in America, England, Europe, the hinterlands of South America, the holy and unholy places of India— wherever he had travelled. Sometimes there was no moral, or any discernable theme, in his stories, the telling made the stories, the telling was the essence of the stories—stories without beginning and end, stories in which the stories themselves were plot, theme and moral. And I can picture him now even as I saw him then. He was always so polite and so unruffled that when he spoke about his years in Scotland, or in the remote interior areas he visited as a Government Medical Officer. I knew he was not really talking about Scotland or South American outposts, but about a universal truth. I felt at times he looked like

Krishna must have looked, calmly delivering the *Bhagavata Gita* to Arjuna before the Great Battle, or like Mahavira or the Buddha under the Pipal Tree.

It always seemed odd that he never had a nurse or receptionist but would himself come to the door of his office which opened into the waiting room, calling softly, "Next," and holding the door open until the patient passed into his office. At a time when Burnham had virtually outlawed the tie in public and official life as a token of the "white man's" colonialism, this man always wore a tie and a white short-sleeved or striped shirt which matched the rim of white hair on his almost bald head.

For several days after I saw his death announcement that morning, I saw him when I looked into the river and at the indistinct west bank; old, muscular, short (he was about five feet two) but very neat and tidy, holding the door open. I saw him at his desk talking, and suddenly one morning it dawned on me that one of the reasons I sat so patiently and listened to him was because I knew he was dying. He had given up on life, and he knew that I knew this. I reminded him of his son in New York, whom he wanted to see, he told me that last time I saw him. He on the other hand reminded me of the visions I always had of what I hoped my father would have been like had he not died when I was two, and had I known him. I was his only link to a country he loved so dearly and in which he had hoped to see his children grow and blossom. He was my link to a world I had heard and read so much of. He had worked for most of his life in all parts of the country, tending to the ill because of a dream and a belief in the goodness of man, and that dream and belief were broken by the world around him, shattered in the world within. Just before he left for New York, just once, I heard him talk politics.

"Black people can't run a cake shop! A country!" It was the only time I saw a sneer on his face—almost a snarl, the snarl of a cornered, faithful dog, grown old, strong yet, but too wise for its master who must kick it out because its silent wisdom and silent resistance to complete manipulation were unbearable. We said our goodbyes and I took one good look around, and outside in the waiting room too, before I went out onto the busy North Road and the haggling of the nearby Bourda Market . . .

Now my memories float up to my tongue. On one hand I seem to hear the worldly-wise *niti* knowledge of Singh's stories, and on the other the Vedanta of Dr Philip Shiv Kumar expounded in the *Panchatantra's* mainframe yet beginningless and endless, and then the two forms of discourse crossing lines and times and types and forms, merging into each other. I can speak about them now but there is no audience and maybe none is needed, as at the time of the beginning of the Sanskrit period, the beginning of the great scribal period of the space we call earth, the end and beginning of eras, the setting down of the Vedas and Upanishads . . . Ah but there, there he is as I look up, holding the door open and softly, politely calling:

"Next . . . "

What more is needed!

Dookie

Dookie would disagree with Soyinka who once said, "I can't enter the mind and body of a woman. Let women write about themselves. Why should they ask me to do that." Dookie had literary aspirations and these he blended with his belief in the transmigration of the soul, in having lived through different ages and different bodies, and in recalling residues of such existences . . .

"The power of the mind's extraordinary—look, see those cane-cutters?" We had all turned and looked out the window at the ash-blackened men cycling toward the sugar factory. Their cutlasses, wedged between the frames of their bicycles, glinted in the afternoon sunshine.

"There are as many small men there as big men. Who do you think works longest, hardest? Those little men. I cut cane too and I can never keep up with the smaller guys. Mind not size or strength. Nothing's impossible!" There was an intensity and passion with which he said it that made us believe. We hung on to Dookie's words, at least I did. He had been teaching at the time, going to university part time where he was involved with the University Students Council, and protesting the government's policy on hiring Rodney at the university while still finding time to work on his parents' farm. In a way, we all admired how he combined the work on the farm with teaching and going to university.

There had been a time, I was in one of the lower forms then, when the school had taken us to see the Hindi film *Hathi Mere Sathi*—"The Elephant Is My Friend"—which came with English subtitles. It was a film that made a great impact on me and my generation who grew up in a rural district of South America among animals, the land, the elements, and felt we could communicate with them all. It was the start of the filmi period of my generation. We couldn't wait for the Saturdays, every other month or so, when our parents would take us "to town" to see the latest Indian movie. My father was more generous but while I was at school, my mother always insisted that we could go to the city only when she, my father or some older relative was with us. The cinema was our living link with an India which was still our mental home. That my parents were Moslems, and that there have since sprung up Islamic countries on the Indian subcontinent, did not matter then. My father could trace his ancestors to Lucknow, and Lucknow was in India, and my mother's people came from somewhere near a place called Rampur, also in the northern Indian state of Uttar Pradesh. The Hindi films we saw did great public relations work for India in preaching Hindu-Moslem-Sikh-Parsi-Christian-and-what-have-you unity, and despite the sometimes gruesome reality of sectarian violence in the news, the filmi world became our reality of India. We were *all* Indians scattered in an alien, distant land and were bewildered at the divisions of Indians at home! In *Sholay* when Rahim died, we all sniffed and sobbed furtively in the cinema, Hindu and Moslem alike. . . . A Moslem, Mohammed Rafi was one of the greatest playback singers in the Hindi film industry and there were great Moslem stars in the Hindi film industry. . .

Dookie and the younger teachers of his generation had said that if schools could take students to see such films as *Mary Poppins* and *To Sir With Love,* then nothing was wrong with *Haathi Mere Saathi.* But if it was this film with its English subtitles, which cracked the barriers which somehow held that only Indians saw Indian films, and that Indian films were "inferior," it was the record-breaking *Bobby,* a film which smashed all box office records in the Caribbean and attracted sell-out crowds, breaking race and colour barriers—at least temporarily. It was a very heady period and perhaps *Bobby* must have influenced me more than I realized. It was about a wealthy upper-class Brahmin boy and a poor Catholic, Goan girl who fell in love, and because of the objections of their parents ran away. At the end the parents consented, love won! It was a variation of the formula movie, with no themes regarding duty, tradition, and religion. It was just a story of young people of different religions and classes being in love, and their love carrying the day. The heroine wore skimpy bathing suits and there were love scenes in libraries. It was a world we could relate to because it dealt with what was starting to happen around us. Hindus were marrying Moslems, Indians were marrying Blacks, Whites, Amerindians.

I suppose we wanted to know about the Other, to test the limits of our societies and we believed in love. For me there was only Dookie. Dookie kept a certain distance between us, yet he was much closer to us than the older teachers, probably because he was just a few years older, and also because of his zest. When there were clean-up days he wouldn't order the boys from the back. He would be the first to pick up a cutlass and start hacking away at the vines on the school fence. We stood around watching, or sometimes helping to clear away the cut vines or grass. Once he fell into a soggy patch near the side fence and his shoes and trousers became all muddy. The boys, knowing of the sogginess there, were deliberately avoiding that section.

"Yuh afraid of mud and water?" he called loudly to the boys. Reluctantly, the boys joined him in clearing that section of the fence, getting their pants muddied in the process. We laughed from our vantage point on the second floor corridor, overlooking the huge picture-perfect Wales Community Centre Cricket Ground.

On that lovely cricket ground, Dookie had elegantly hit a burly Black fast bowler from Stewartville Secondary School for three consecutive boundaries in one over. Our entire school was there to cheer the school team on, and two buses packed with students and teachers had come from Stewartville to support their team. It was a time when the gamesmaster could play on the school cricket team and the games-mistress on the girls rounders team. It was a time when the years of Black racism and massively rigged elections, police and military in-timidation and violence, had finally touched us in that quiet South American countryside. Some of the boys were scared of the speed and bounce of the burly Black fast bowler whose reputation had preceded him. Our school team was comprised entirely of Indians while the Ste-wartville team consisted mainly of Blacks. After the first two overs, two batsmen were already back in the pavilion and we had not scored a single run. There was a tension in the air especially as some specta-tors felt that the bowler was "pelting" and not bowling. A complaint, lodged with the umpires and the captain of the opposing team, was disallowed and the Stewartville students in the pavilion started boo-ing. Another wicket fell and Dookie who normally batted lower down came to the wicket.

In that first over Dookie faced, he struck the fast bowler twice through extra cover and froze in position, not even bothering to move from his crease, arrogantly certain that the ball would strike the boundary. It did. But it was only when he square cut the next ball for a third consecutive boundary that everyone erupted in applause. It is one of those innings you never forget. Dookie hit a boundary in every over, scored 107 runs and was the last man out. We cheered him all the way to the pavilion and the boys lifted him off the field. I could not even get close to him but I remembered his mind-matter pro-nouncements then! There were all sorts of metaphors there . . .

There were times when he looked at me so deeply and meaning-fully, that I felt he must have known how I felt for him. At such times, I felt that he felt the same way about me. He loved the trees, the wind in the trees, the birds, the rain, the dewdrops sparkling on the trees towering just above us on the nearby riverbank which kept the mighty Demerara River at bay, and he nurtured and encouraged this love in us. But most of the time Dookie rarely seemed to notice me, at least no more than any of the other girls in our literature class. Nothing happened, as I hoped and dreamed that it would, but it did not matter. I had time and the odds were on my side as we lived in the same village.

I left school at a time and place where girls who did not do well enough, or were not permitted to get a job or go on to university, got married or went to Miss Singh's Secretarial school. We saw nothing wrong with this. It was the way it was and we worked within that system as best as we could. Later we came to North America and things changed. Then, it was beautiful in its own way, less complicated, less combative and sometimes, just sometimes, I wish I were back there in that commercial school and in that time and place.

Miss Singh was very strict. She allowed no fancy makeup and dressing up. She said we went to her school because our parents paid a lot of money for us to learn some useful skills, and that was what we would do or we could go to another school—there would be no hanky-panky. Girls in the uniform of her school who were seen with boys in various "love spots" and reported to her had their parents called in to the office, and were sometimes expelled. It was well known that the girls who went to her school did well at all levels of the Pitman's Examinations, and went on to get jobs in every government department and private company that mattered, so few girls were willing to risk expulsion.

I met Dookie on the ferry one afternoon after classes. We were both going home, he from a lecture at the university and I from Miss Singh's, and that was when it really started. We stood up in a little doorway just inside the bow on the crowded ferry, high above the large waves of the Demerara and talked in spurts. Over the heads of other commuters, we occasionally caught glimpses of the Atlantic and beyond. From then on we met regularly in the Gardens almost directly across from the school. As everyone in the city knew the grey skirt and white blouse of Miss Singh's Secretarial School, there was change and change again! We nestled in the shade of huge cannonball trees or behind shrubs, talked, stole kisses, made plans for the future . . .

One day as we sat facing the bandstand, he got up suddenly and ran up onto the bandstand. He could never really sit still for long. There was always that bursting energy in him and you could feel it.

"Indira Gandhi once stood here. Right here," he said when I joined him.

"O, I was small—so," he drew a line just below my breasts. "Ajee knew a woman who worked here and she got us in—god—I have never seen so many people, so many Indians, outside, inside. All I knew was that this was a great woman, the Prime Minister of India and it was a great moment in my life to see her and hear her. The Kabaka was probably there, after all he was the Prime Minister but I saw only her, felt that only she was important. I don't remember anything of her speech. But I can feel her standing here, talking, waving to us. A sari flapping in the wind. Brilliant sunshine, the crowd . . . A great woman, a great Indian."

"Well, isn't he her father," I said pointing to the statue of the Mahatma at the back of the Gardens.

"No. The name Gandhi she got from her husband—a Feroze Gandhi—not really related to the Mahatma. Her father was Pandit Nehru," he said, his eyes fixed on the statue of the Mahatma.

"Really!" Was all I could manage through my shock and surprise. I felt humbled because I was mistaken but also excited. Feroze was a popular Moslem name in our community and suddenly Indira Gandhi rose in my estimation. She became something of an idol. All sorts of thoughts were tumbling through my head. Two months after that meeting on the ferry, Dookie graduated from the university. He was the best graduating student and won all sorts of prizes. His photograph appeared in the Sunday papers and everyone in our village was excited—even my parents. Dookie was after all "a village bhai." I think what endeared him to everyone was that he continued working on his parents' farm as usual while school was closed that August, and that cane season he cut cane too. Miss Singh's School had closed for the holidays and we hardly met. That August seemed to drag on forever.

I was impatient for a glimpse of him. On the long thin road which ran through our village one hears a car, a tractor and especially a motorcycle's engine a long way off. Except there in South America, I have seen few villages like it. The road was straight as an arrow running west from the Demerara river and ending at the conservancy near the savannah. It was seven miles long. There were houses on the northern side of it and the farmlands. Next to it, on the south, was a huge canal which the Dutch had had their slaves dig centuries ago. On the far side of that canal was a wide dam and a dry-weather road lined by a row of houses, then the canefields started. The row of houses on either side of the Canal and road was just one house deep. Very few people had a car and almost all of the cars in the village were "taxis." A few people had motorcycles and these were almost all men who worked on the sugar estate. The estate provided trail motorcycles for the rough terrain of the estate, and I have heard my father and brother talk of the motorcycles. They said the estate administrators and the staff preferred the 100cc trail Hondas because these were the most hardy and durable for the tough estate rides. Kamal, my brother, who worked on the estate had a Honda and he was very proud of it. He had purchased it from the estate at cost. It was one of the benefits of having "position" on the estate.

Dookie had a 250cc Yamaha and I had long memorized the smooth thin buzz of its engine. It was the only motorcycle of its kind in the village and was distinctly different from the heavy, throaty Hondas. I had heard Kamal saying that Dookie's Yamaha could outrun anything on wheels in the village but once it came off the road, on to the trail and especially in the rainy weather, it was no good. I liked Dookie's motorcycle best because it did not have those huge gaps between the wheel and the fenders, which moreover were not the small plastic types. They were of chrome and positioned just above the wheels. The gas tank, the seat and the handle bar were very streamlined. Those two months when school was closed, I lived only for the sound of Dookie's Yamaha. As soon as I heard it in the distance, I would hustle as unobtrusively as possible to our verandah or to a window, or if Kamal and his friends were not there, onto our bridge. Dookie lived at the far end of the village to the west so he had to pass our house when he was going to town or leaving the village, going to the estate office or even to the only hardware store in the village.

When school reopened in September, Dookie was transferred to teach at St Joseph's, a school in the northeastern end of the city, so it was easier to meet in town or on the ferry. We thought that it was best we let our parents know that we wanted to get married. I was scared that sooner or later someone would see us and tell my parents—Dookie did not care but he hated the hide-and-seek manner in which we met.

"So dah wha bina happen—dah wha mih sen yuh school fah!" my mother started screaming when I told her. "Yuh nah want Muslim Bhai? Wha wrang with Shamin?" Shamin's parents were very wealthy and he was not unattractive.

"Nah easy gyaal! Yuh a Muslim an Dookie Hindu." My father spoke less vehemently than my mother. I was stunned. I had expected some support from my father.

"What wrang with yuh gyaal?" my mother screamed again.

"I love Dookie and Dookie love me," I said defiantly.

"And what yuh know 'bout love Shaira?" my father asked.

"Dhis na bout love. Ahbi time we nah see wan a'nather till nikka!"

"Maa dhis na lang time!" Kamal said. I had not expected any support from Kamal. Kamal went to masjid every Friday and was learning Urdu and Arabic.

"Bhai, yuh kepp outta dhis," Ma said sharply to him then to me, 'Leh mih talk dhis with yuh daadi!'

The next day my mother said flatly, "Gyaal abhi na 'gree fuh dhis wedding! Yuh know abhi papers near come from 'merika! If yuh get marrid yuh lef back yah. Yuh na see Dookie a' marry yuh fuh get to 'merika! Use yuh head. If he love yuh he guh do anything fuh yuh—he a wait till yuh get thru' to 'merika—well abhi a see soon if he really love yuh. Kamal gaan fuh he!" I was faintly conscious that Kamal had gone somewhere on his motorcycle. I soon heard both motorcycles coming.

"So yuh love Shaira?" my mother asked aggressively as soon as

Dookie sat on the chair in the verandah.

"Yes. We want get married." The relaxed, confident way he said it made me want to walk up to him and kiss him right there. I felt there was no way they could refuse now.

"Yuh know ahbi near fuh get through to Amerika?" My father asked.

"No," he hesitated and looked at me. I had never mentioned it to him.

"Amin seh suh every year fuh four years now!" I blurted out.

"Shut up gyaal!" my mother said fiercely. "If al-yuh marry she get lef back! Things hard hey! Dhis na abhi country—dhis a blackman country!"

"Shaira mai an me think yuh and Shaira could do Nikka! No signing no paypa, so Shaira still get thru to Amerika and she could come back an duh a legal wedding afta." My father said. It was a solution. There was a pause and we all looked at Dookie. He looked at me then at my father and had started nodding his head in agreement.

Then my mother added, "An' we gat wan nice name fuh yuh!"

"What!" Dookie said sharply.

"Yuh know fuh do Nikka yuh gat to turn Muslim," my father said.

"I love you," Dookie said looking at me, "I am not asking you to become Hindu." He turned to my father. "No—don't try to convert me!" He stood up. It was the first time I saw Dookie angry.

"See how he love yuh!" my mother hissed, "Dhis cyant wuk!"

Dookie nodded and left. We had already arranged our meeting the next week. But that Sunday was to be more eventful than I expected. We were sitting under the house about to eat dinner when Dookie's mother came striding into the yard.

"Suh Golin wah thing dhis mih hear. Let dhi pickney dhem get marrid if dhem like wan a'nather. Dhis a different time! Nowadays chiren na stupid like abhi time! Golin abhi gu to school together, abhi eat a'matti house, abhi wuk a'backdam together, abhi a Indian! Wah dhis thing 'bout Muslim? Yuh wan turn mih son Muslim! Wha wang with Hindu? Hindu na good fuh yuh daatha? Yuh fuget yuh own muddha bina Hindu? Yuh want mek mih son Muslim like how yuh aja dhem mek yuh mumma turn Muslim?"

"Gyaal dha wan lang time. Thing different now!" my mother managed feebly. I had not known until then that my grandmother was Hindu. I had only known her as Nani Waheeda. Waheeda was a Muslim name!

"Yuh right. Dha a lang time when evry Hindu marry Muslim, he gat fuh turn Muslim! Careful this nah backfire Golin gyaal—wha guh round come round!" Dookie's mother stormed out of our yard. But nothing changed. I was two months short of my eighteenth birthday and my parents refused to agree. Dookie's parents would not agree once my parents did not agree—even after my birthday. Dookie just said one day that we should go and get married if I still wanted to. I wanted to. I had just received the results of the Pitman Intermediate Exams and I had got a distinction. It was a Friday. We went to the General Post Office and signed the papers and then we went to the Pegasus Hotel. It was the first time I had gone to the Pegasus, the first time I had gone to any hotel. Only the next morning it started to sink in. We had run away, eloped. We had not told any of our parents and I became apprehensive. Dookie said that we should spend the weekend and not bother about our parents. We had our lives to live. I felt that he was right. That Sunday afternoon when we finally went to our village, I cried as we rode past my parents' house and I wanted to wave to Kamal who was on the verandah but we passed too quickly. Word of what had happened had already spread through the village. When we rode into Dookie's yard I was nervous.

Dookie's father shouted as we approached the yard, "What nansene yuh duh bhai? What nansense dhis!"

"Pa dhis mih wife," Dookie said quietly as he cut the engine.

"Mih na gree widh dhis thing!" Dookie's father shouted angrily again.

"Pa dhis done a'ready—if yuh want we could leave . . . "

"Dookie Bhai, why why . . . " his mother called from the kitchen rushing out into the yard, "yuh na tell nobady nuthin—Bhai mih worry . . . "

"Ma we marry . . . "

His mother paused, shook her head, straightened and suddenly came up to me and held my arm, "Come gyaal come . . . And no more arguing now Pa—dhis done a'ready!" We were halfway through eating when Ma, my father and Kamal came storming into the yard. I thought there might be a fight.

"Suh yuh kidnap mih daughta!" Ma shouted. People gathered on the road and some neighbours came in the yard. Dookie got up.

"Dookie and Pa sit down—don't seh nothin," Dookie's mother said.

"Suh dhis a what yuh encourage mih daughta fuh do," Ma screamed again.

"Golin stap shoutin. And come yah and listin good—and stap takin stupidness! Mih ole man an me nah 'gree fuh dhis thing, but it happen. It happen a'ready. Yuh want mih put mih own son on dhi road? Yuh wan mih put Shaira on dhi road. She a yuh daughta. She a mih daughta now to! Dhem gat to live someway!"

"Gyaal why yuh shame mih suh," Ma rushed up to me and Dookie stood up. Pa rushed in the yard as though towards Dookie and I started sobbing. They all started looking at me. There was silence.

"Ma . . . " I said crying out to her.

"Mih nah yuh Ma. Yuh bring shame to mih. Yuh nah mi daughta. Mih na gat wan daughta from today . . ." And Ma strode out of the yard. I cried for nights afterwards until later I felt bitter and angry with my parents.

We stayed with Dookie's parents until the hand-holding scandal spread through the village. I suppose it couldn't work for us there in our little village. There was too much going against us, and in a way it was Dookie against the world, though I could not see it then. If we went for a walk in the afternoon, Dookie would hold my hands. Sometimes he would kiss me lightly on my face when we got up on Savis Dam, overlooking the savannah. It was beautiful in the sunset as we looked to the savannah in the west. In the rainy season, when the conservancy overflooded its banks, the sun shone like gold on the dark water, from which protruded the long stalks of grass dancing in the wind. There was water for as far as the eye could see, throwing up that liquidy evening gold we loved. It was better than anything I had ever seen in any movie. I had lived in our village all my life and had never seen this beauty in the wildness beyond it, never even seen it from a distance till those evenings he took me on the high dam on the edge of the savannah. We would hold hands, stand close together with his arm around me in the dusk as he told me how beautiful it was when he had gone into the savannah, and into the forest beyond. Often, we just stood in silence, admiring it from our vantage point.

Dookie's father blew up one night. The whole village was talking about the new "public romancing"!

"Yuh eva see yuh mai and me hold han anytime, anyway—or kissup all over dhe place. Yuh nah gat no respect fuh nobady bhai!" he shouted at Dookie as we entered the yard after one of our evening strolls.

Dookie did not respond and we went quietly to our room. Dookie said that we should get a place in the city and move out of the village. I was glad. The tension was still there and whenever we had to pass my parents' place, I would feel all queasy inside, now there was the tension at his parents'.

We were lucky. One of Dookie's professors had a vacant apartment in his house in Queenstown, not far from the Indian Cultural Centre. It was a beautiful apartment in a quiet and lovely residential area. In it we spent some of the best times in our lives and I started learning about the very combative and political Dookie. Dookie supported both the WPA and the PPP until one of his friends said, "The PPP is a waste. Jagan can't do nothing. Only Rodney can get Burnham out! We gat to support Rodney!"

"Why?" Dookie asked.

"Because Jagan can't get the black people support and he too old. Even many Indians don't support Jagan. Yuh see yuself how many Indians support Rodney!"

"That's the racism! Black people can't support Jagan because Jagan is Indian and he going against "one-a-dhem"! Burhman is still "one-a-dhem." Rodney is also "one-a-dhem," even if he go against Burnham. Racism! That's the problem with this country! Not class and capitalism-socialism nonsense, but racism!"

I followed from the sidelines, and I felt that Dookie was right. Sometimes he took me to political meetings where the tension was always unbearable. I always felt that anything could happen at any moment. There was something exciting about the period. I was there with Dookie, at the meeting on Middle street near Miss Singh's school, when Rodney compared Burnham to the man with the reverse Midas touch—a man whose touch turned everything to shit. I had never seen so many people in my life at a meeting, and there were police all around. But we laughed and cheered nervously when Rodney made the comparison.

I was still going to Miss Singh's in the day so I could do the advanced Pitman's Examination. In the afternoon, I went to the Indian Cultural Centre where I had started doing Indian classical dance. It was something I had always wanted to do. Dookie did vocal music. We went to the various Indian concerts, Phagwah fairs and the Diwali motorcades. There were the walks in the National Park or in the Botanical Gardens among the symmetry, colour and poetry of well cut grass, blooming flowers, birds, sunsets; there were the dashes for shelter in unexpected showers; there were the evening rides to the seawall, looking at the sun go down on the Atlantic or the magic of the city lighting up from the Kitty groyne when there were no blackouts; there were the nights we sat on the seawall and cuddled up as the moon rose, in front of us on the Atlantic, as the night-lit ships were entering and leaving the Demerara River—the huge, laden ocean-going ships could only cross the channel bar at high tide—Dookie would slip in from his storehouse of information; and there were the long rides along the East Coast, and the overnight trips to visit some of his friends on the Corentyne and Essequibo Coasts. Everything was strange and new to me. Life had become full because of Dookie and there was always something to look forward to. I suppose I knew that if it were not for him, I would not have gone to half those places, met all those people.

As Dookie was Hindu, I accompanied him even on Sundays to the Kitty Mandir or the Gandhi Youth Bhavan. I felt at first that it was a small price for all he gave me. I wanted to please him but I also felt at ease in his Hindu world.

When I mentioned it, he said casually, "An ancestral memory—an ancient instinct. Perhaps every Indian Muslim is a Hindu at heart—or what we call a Hindu. Before the coming of the Turks to India, before Buddhism or Jainism even, all Indians belonged to what has come to be known as Hinduism today. The Muslims did wholesale conversion with the sword and a decadent caste system helped . . ." This fired me to read up Indian history at the Indian Cultural Centre Library. And I felt that, as usual, Dookie was right. Where, when had he learnt all of this?

At the nearby Empire and Liberty cinemas, which showed only Hindi films, we went almost every weekend to see old and new movies. I loved the opening-night shows, the crowds and the long lineups. So many Indians! But we also went to the other movies occasionally—the American or English films, the "classics" or movies based on some novel Dookie had read or studied or heard about. There was nobody to tell Dookie or me about holding hands or kissing in public or private. Our village on the West Bank seemed so far away until Kamal came one day to say that they had finally got through to go to America. Ma still didn't want to see me and that hurt. Kamal said that Pa felt that Dookie was using me to get to America and Pa didn't want to see me either, but Kamal said he felt Ma was wavering, that she would change. I think Kamal admired Dookie for going against all the traditions. Kamal said he would write from New York, and his visit affected us. Dookie wondered about his own parents. With Ma and Pa gone to New York there was a sort of emptiness. Though they had wanted nothing to do with us, we always knew that they were there, and we had felt that with time there would be a reconciliation.

I was glad when Dookie suggested that we visit his parents that Diwali. When we entered the yard, it was as though nothing had happened. His parents were very happy to see us and insisted that we stay the holiday weekend. After that weekend, his mother or father visited us in Queenstown every month. Every time they came, they brought whatever fruits and vegetables that were in season, and provisions too. This was a great help to us.

But the politics soon overshadowed everything. Rodney's assassination shocked the entire country. The Death Squad became more active and visible. Dookie had gone to the meeting at the Kitty Market Square alone when the Death Squad started beating people at random. The huge crowd breaking up in disarray and panic was the most terrifying part. He said more people were trampled and injured by the fleeing crowd than by the goons. At the next meeting, as soon as the goons arrived, they were set upon and thrashed—some had their arms broken and ran into the nearby police station. But at the next political meeting on the old railway line, the goons sought revenge. The meeting was a disaster. The main speaker, one of the leaders of the WPA, was targeted by the Death Squad and he barely escaped with his life. It was later said he was saved from certain death when he hid in a dark fowl pen in somebody's backyard. The President, in his next "Address to the Nation" openly mocked the WPA and the opposition. At every opposition meeting the goons were there. One meeting ended in disarray, and Dookie and a number of others were captured and beaten, taken more than forty miles away on the deserted Linden Highway, stripped of their footwear, blackjacked on the soles of their feet then dumped in the dark forest. I couldn't sleep that night. I thought that Dookie too was murdered. By the time he turned up the next day, dishevelled, bruised, barefoot, his parents had arrived, having received the message I had sent.

"Dhis a serious business! Yuh na need university degree to see murder! Dhem blackman dhis mean fuh kill anybady who show opposition—dhem neva give up power!" His father argued.

"Dookie come home—leave dhis stupidness . . ." his mother pleaded.

"Yuh can't fight guns with words—If yuh want fight get guns. Dhem blackman only frighten bullets in dhe rrass . . . like '62 . . . " His father said.

"No. We gat plenty lan. Come home. Na matta wha happen yuh can't starve. An yuh can't think only 'bout yuself. What 'bout Shaira?" His mother pleaded.

Dookie nodded in agreement but said nothing. He became quieter and I knew that inside he was seething. When they left, he muttered almost to himself, "Always the family!" It was after he went to the next meeting that I started receiving the menacing phone calls. When I told him about the calls, he told me to pack up some clothes. We went that very night to our village, to his parents. They were glad that we had come. We stayed all weekend. Dookie stayed up late with his father one night and they went in to the Backdam. They came back early in the morning just before dawn. When he went to teach that Monday, he was given a transfer notice from the Ministry of Education. He had two weeks to take up his new posting at a school in Kwakwani, a remote bauxite mining town one hundred miles up the Berbice River, in the bush, and more than two hundred miles away. He left for work the next day and to make arrangements to clear out the apartment. When he came home, and after dinner, he and his father went for another walk in the night. The next day he left early for the city and he came home late. He went straight upstairs and beckoned us up. He had two tickets for Canada and the tax exits. We would leave the next day, on the Thursday morning flight for Toronto. We would travel light, he said. While we packed, his father went to make arrangements for a taxi. Dookie went out alone to the end of the village, to the conservancy dam looking over the savannah and the bush.

And as the sun went down on the grass of the savannah and the thin line of trees marking the edge of the forest, I felt something change in Dookie. He returned without his edge and spark. For me it was different. The rash of activity, the novelty and change energized me. I was sad at leaving it all behind but more than anything else, I was excited that I would be leaving the country, going to another land, starting over. I suppose I had always wanted to go, ever since my eldest brother had gone to New York many years ago and kept promising that soon we would join him, that we could do anything we wanted there, that in North America the sky was the limit: and Toronto was just north of New York.

II

It was a year before we got permits to work in Canada and in that year we lived with Dookie's aunt, Madhu, and her husband. I looked after the two younger girls, taking them to and from the nearby school and helping them with their projects. On the weekends, once the weather was good, Dookie's aunt and her husband showed us around Toronto and Ontario. I looked forward to those weekends and the trips to the parks, the nearby Scarborough Bluffs, the malls, the CN Tower, the Science Centre, a hundred and one places. His aunt, who was teaching in a Catholic school, pointed out that Dookie would have little problem getting into the teaching system. She said I could get a clerical job while I went to university. There was so much to look forward to! I missed much of what was happening to Dookie in this first year except that he was restless, morose and impatient for the work-permit. Looking after the two girls gave me a sense of being useful and of earning our keep at his aunt's. I think it bothered him more that it did me, that he was not contributing in any way, especially as our almost nonexistent income made movement for him limited. Aunt Madhu and I got along well, and I think from the first night we met at Pearson Airport something clicked. I knew that we were going to get along, but Dookie was apprehensive and uncertain.

Aunt Madhu's husband often worked double shifts and was very reserved. He seemed under constant pressure and Dookie felt that this was because he was displeased with our presence in the house. I never knew how much this affected Dookie, but I knew that he tried not to get in his uncle's way. It was different with me and his aunt Madhu.

She was very independent and was glad to have me with her. The two of us and the younger girls were always going some place or the other. That first summer Dookie prowled the downtown areas and the libraries, and once the weather was good he was rarely inside. I enjoyed the daytime talk shows on television, and it was through these shows and Aunt Madhu that I became conscious of the women's rights movement. Aunt Madhu wore shorts to go shopping in the summer and bathing suits when we went picnicking on the lake Simcoe beach, and she bought shorts and a swimsuit for me. I had never before worn a swimsuit or shorts. Dookie hated swimsuits and shorts—he felt that all this "nakedness" was vulgar.

His aunt teased him, "So what about men who wear shorts too! Is that vulgar? Dookie Dhis is Canada! If you don't come to grips with this society you'll lose out—be left behind. We have a right to do what we like just like you men—buy the things we like—we earn our money! Ha! Lighten up."

"And look we've bought shorts for you too!" I added and everybody laughed. He too laughed but I knew he wasn't pleased. His aunt was right, as were all those women I heard on the talk shows, passionately and eloquently talking about women's rights and showing how the society and men discriminated against us.

When we got our work permits Dookie was happy until he read the fine print. Teaching was one of the restricted areas of employment. I was lucky. Aunt Madhu knew a lawyer who, just then, needed an office assistant. Even though I had no prior work experience, Aunt Madhu's recommendation was more than good enough. The lawyer, Stephnie was a white Canadian-born woman who said that of all the employees she had had, those from Guyana and the Philippines were the most conscientious. Dookie was not so fortunate. In the first months he could get no job in the banks or insurance companies. He was always too qualified for the few entry-level positions available, and even though he was willing to accept them he was bypassed. He got a job in a furniture factory. I was earning two dollars an hour more than he was, and I had a full five-day work week, while he sometimes only got three days' work.

Aunt Madhu suggested that we could rent her basement when she finished fixing it up but Dookie found all sorts of excuses. The rent Aunt Madhu asked was a bargain, and she said that it would give us a chance to save money. I agreed with her but Dookie was silent. In private we argued about this. He did not say it outright but he resented that I was so much influenced by Aunt Madhu. He told Aunt Madhu laughingly that he had never lived in "a hole in the ground" and would not if he could help it.

We got a one-bedroom apartment on Don Mills near the Fairview Mall. Stephnie's office was in the Mall so I just had to walk across Don Mills Road to work while Dookie had to travel to Scarborough. I don't think that he minded. It meant that he left home before me and came home after me, and by the time he came home, I had already washed the dishes and made dinner. He resented those days when he was not working and had to wash the dishes and begin dinner, and I resented that he resented this. Before coming to Canada he had never done any of this. Before we were married his mother did most of it and then I did it all for him. I pointed out that at a time when he was the sole income earner and I was at home all day, it was alright that I did all the cooking and housework. Now we both went out to work and I worked longer than he, earned more than he, and so he could not leave all the housework to me. I began to feel that I was his servant. I began to resent him.

It was around this time he found out that he still needed to do a few more credits to be able to teach in any Ontario school, whenever we got our Landed Immigrant status. He went back to university. We had decided that we would not start a family until we got our Landed status so while he was busy at university and studying, I had decided to get my driver's licence. Aunt Madhu gave me driving practice when she had time. I got my license before him and I felt a sense of accomplishment and satisfaction in this. I felt that I too should go to university and get a degree. I did not want to be stuck as a secretary all my life. I had just completed my pre-university course when we got our

Landed Immigrant status.

The counsellor at York University suggested that I do Women's Studies, which was a new degree programme being offered by the university. Working with Stephanie and looking at all those divorce cases in which women were battered and abused made me want to do something about it all. I wanted to do law but it would take forever, and besides, I felt that Stephanie and lawyers, while doing important things for women, were approaching the problem from the back end, trying to make a pain easier to live with. I believed in preventive medicine, tackling the root of the problem. I enroled for Women's Studies.

Dookie was flustered when I told him.

"What about law?" He asked.

"A degree's a degree," I reminded him. At first I felt intimidated with the long essays and asked him to help me with the grammar and organization of the material. He had done English for his degree and was teaching it in high school. When he read my papers he made fun.

"Women and men are not physically equal," he smirked.

"It doesn't mean we don't deserve equal rights!" I retorted.

"Sure you deserve equal rights but that still does not make us equal."

"That's a myth—one small biological difference does not give men the right to subjugate women . . . and men have been doing that from the beginning, that is the reason of all religion. Look at Islam and Hinduism too—all religion! Why can't women become priests?"

"So that's the reason you have stopped going to pujas!" He said. It irritated me how he was able to mock me and then escape from the issue at hand by drawing on some example which led to something else. In our discussions he moved from topic to topic with ease, relating everything to the topic in a roundabout way. Nothing was exempt for him.

"No. Because of my studies I don't have as much time now! So why no women priests in Hinduism?"

"Because a few men wanted power over everybody else—other men as well as women! It is not a man-woman issue but a matter of power. If and when we get more women priests, women will have the power in their sects over other women and men. No different from the men priests . . . "

"All religion and philosophy are the same—designed to subjugate women!" I retorted.

"No. At least not in Hinduism. One Vedic concept is that all forms of manifest energy is an embodiment of the female principle, the Shakti. The only 'male' principle is 'god' or the all powerful, pure cosmic consciousness. And thus even Shiva is not 'man' but half-man, half-woman. You know the story of the great Hindu saint, Mira—I forget you did not have the Hindu background . . . "

I resented his reminder and the mockery.

". . . She was a great bhakta and these brahmins refused to admit her to this ashram where the great male intellectuals of the day prayed, worshipped and carried out their intellectual discussions—just because she was a woman. So she told the disciple who refused her admittance to tell his guru that from what she knew, and from the Vedas, there was only one male principle— 'god.' Humbled, the guru himself came to the door, apologised and admitted her to the ashram and the gathering. There were several other great women saints in Indian life. It is no coincidence that Hindus worship god alternately, simultaneously and sometimes only in the female form as Uma, Saraswati, Durga, Parvati, etc. The point is, you can't condemn an entire religious philosophy if you don't know that philosophy. Philosophy is the most concrete human endeavour, formulated from the society, based on convictions, not skin-deep words, or based on the misguided, misinterpreted practices of a particular sect!"

"You're just trying to justify it all . . ." But I felt humbled, put down and more determined to pursue what I was doing. It was what, as one lecturer had pointed out, men had always been doing to make women feel inferior. Yet I felt Dookie was right in one respect; knowledge was important, research and learning the facts were important, and I felt that my courses were an important step in this direction.

When I came home from classes one evening, he said my mother had called from New York. She left her address and phone number.

"Well, aren't you going to call her?" He asked.

"No." I was not so much angry with my mother as surprised and shocked at the suddenness.

"Why?" he asked, surprised.

"You forget she disowned me! She didn't even tell us that she got through to New York . . . "

"She said it in anger. She was quite nice on the phone. And she's still your mother . . . "

"Dookie, don't push me, don't bother me. I'm not ready for her, I'm not ready for this . . . !"

Another two months elapsed before Kamal called from New York and we talked for a long time. He said Ma and Pa were separated! Pa was having an affair with one of his young, distant cousins and had beaten ma. The separation shocked me. I called her.

When she answered and called my name, she started crying. I too started crying. Dookie went outside on to the balcony.

When he came in after an hour, I was still on the phone with Ma and I was just telling her, "Divorce him—he can't treat you like this. No man has the right to hit a woman. And he hit you before too, I remember. I knew all those times when we were growing up. And if he ever shows up near your apartment call the cops immediately. He'll not change. Divorce him . . . No I can't come now. I've got exams and two papers to hand in. Not till September. And change the door locks—get the super to change it and don't let him in. How long will his money last? How long will his young girls want him? You've to get on with your life . . . " When I put down the phone I was shaking and when Dookie came and put his arm around me, I told him everything. The words tumbled out of me. Ma had worked in a cosmetics factory since she had arrived in New York. She was now a line supervisor in the factory. Pa worked occasionally, was always drinking and chasing after women, gambling or just looking at the TV. He was lucky and often won considerable amounts from his gambling and he felt that this entitled him to special status. He hardly helped in the home. Ma had to have counselling. She had had a breakdown and now she had diabetes. And I wanted to see her. Kamal was married and hardly visited her as he was living in Jersey City and my older brother had moved to Florida . . .

"Well go. I hate New York," Dookie said.

"You don't have to go if you don't want to!" I said sharply, without thinking. Dookie had always hated New York and America long before we had come to Canada. The Americans felt they were the salt of the earth and his courses on American literature and the American involvement in the fiasco of the '60s and in the continued mess of Guyana politics only deepened his dislike. I forgot all of that in his remark. I only heard: "I do not want to go so you should not want to go."

"Alright, alright, take it easy . . . when are you thinking of going?" he asked.

"I don't know. I don't have a break until September and I have so much reading and work to do . . . "

"I think your work load is too much. You work and go part time to university—it's not easy. When I did it back home I was teaching so I had time—two months in August, two weeks at Christmas, three weeks at Easter plus all those school holidays. It was easier and I was not married. You know, we hardly spend time together. When you come home it is straight to your books and you don't want me disturbing you, and when you come in I'm already in bed or vice versa. We hardly even make love . . . How do you want to get pregnant?" He asked.

"That's because I don't get anything from it and I am too tired and you only want sex when I want to sleep . . ." I had told him once that when I was asleep he was never to wake me for sex.

"I'm not a machine Shaira. When I'm stimulated you are studying and when we go to bed it takes a while for me to relax, only then I can get my sex drive up. Sex is like studying, like anything else. If we don't make time for it: and I don't mean just the act, then it can't happen. You think I can jump in bed and get it up right away! The spark has to be nurtured—I live with you for years and see you day in day out—the glitter goes out. I'm sure it's the same for you . . . "

"So what are you saying, you want another woman too, you want me to stop university—or both?"

"No I'm just suggesting you reduce the amount of courses you do . . . "

"It will take too long. And that's fine for you. You already have a degree. What have I got? . . . "

"Forget it," he said. "There's a long weekend next month, in May, why don't you go for the weekend. You can get a Friday night flight after work and come back Monday afternoon or Monday night. Wouldn't affect your classes." This quick thinking and spontaneity which had made me fall in love with Dookie was surfacing again. In the weeks leading up to that first trip to New York, life seemed intoxicating. There were the phone calls back and forth and the hunting around for gifts for Ma, Kamal and his wife. Kamal said Ma and I had to spend a night with them in Jersey City. Dookie, though he was not going, seemed just as excited about it all and I felt in love with him all over again. I knew that he could make the trip if he wanted, and realized that he was giving me time to be alone with Ma, that he knew I wanted to be alone with her after all these years, and after so much that had happened since I got married.

It rained that weekend in New York and we spent most of the time indoors, in Ma's apartment. It seemed cramped and dark and I put it down to the overcast weather. We went to bed late that first night and got up late the next morning. The stories of Pa, of her life since I got married, snippets of her childhood all bubbled out of her. And she wanted to show off New York to me: this was a fairly decent neighbourhood but you still had to be careful; O that is the Tri-Borough bridge, through the drizzle, with its arching rail lights. Across there is Manhattan. The planes going down, just over the bridge, are heading into La Guardia Airport. That was where you came in. Kennedy Airport is just to the south near Jamaica Bay there . . .

If I had not studied a map of New York in Toronto, I would have had no idea of what she was talking about. I silently thanked Dookie.

Two weeks before my trip he went to the bookstore and bought a detailed map of New York. He located the street where Ma lived and marked it for me and then he went to the library and obtained books about the history and the neighbourhoods of contemporary New York City. I did not have much time to read the books so as we drove to the supermarket and shopped, he told me about the history and neighbourhoods, the places of interest in concise summaries.

Ma admitted she was wrong about Dookie. She said that I was lucky in Dookie, and I felt a little pride and glow in me for Dookie, and perhaps I boasted a little about Dookie—about how helpful he was around the home, how considerate, and I told her about Aunt Madhu. Ma knew Aunt Madhu. They went to school together with Dookie's mother. We started making connections again and I suggested that she visit Toronto.

Her accent had changed. There was a foreign sounding lilt to it. She too had changed. She was no longer the staid, conservative woman I knew. There was a time when I was in high school when she would not even let me go to the cinema alone or wear trousers. She had cut her hair and bleached it a sandy brown. When she met me at the airport, looking slim and chic in her jeans, I didn't recognize her at first and back in her apartment she had changed into shorts as she put on the airconditioner. This was a woman who had never worn pants in Guyana and who, like most women and men of her generation, often walked around barefoot in the village, wore long dresses and a rumaal on her head. The transformation was remarkable. She looked ten years younger and she joked that she did it all to hold Pa.

"He said, I turning 'white' woman!" she said "He hated it!" She started sobbing and I remembered Dookie.

"Yes, he want the woman you were before—a woman he could control!" There was much we had to tell each other and when Kamal and his wife came on Saturday night, it rained heavily. We did not go to New Jersey and he and his wife ended up staying the night with us. We started making plans for my return visit and plans for them visiting us in Toronto. Kamal took us for a drive through Manhattan; under the

Empire State Building, past the Waldorf-Astoria Hotel, and Grand Central Station, the New York Public Library, the United Nations building: the Statue of Liberty hidden in the rain and mist. I recognized a few places I saw in movies and the bridges over the East River. There was something about Manhattan that I liked. After all the negative comments by Dookie, I had half expected a very run down, shabby and fearsome place.

The weekend went well but I was happy to return to Toronto and to see Dookie. It was the first time since we had gotten married that we had spent any time away from each other. I missed him. I think he missed me too. Pearson Airport was bright and airy after New York and it was only when we came off the 401 that I realized the difference between Toronto and New York: it was in the trees and vegetation—greenery. But none of this prepared me for the shock I received when we entered our apartment. Sun was streaming through the large windows and the cream carpet and the white tiles on the floor seemed extraordinarily clean and cheery. It seemed Dookie had thoroughly cleaned the apartment in my absence. Our "honeymoon" lasted a month. I had not felt so close to him since before we had arrived in Canada and l told him everything about Ma, Pa and Kamal. Dookie listened attentively.

Ma phoned soon after I arrived home.

"Ma has filed for a divorce," I told him after she put down the phone.

"And that is the best course!" Dookie said quietly. He was looking out the window and did not turn to face me. That disconcerted me.

"Yes. He will not change!"

"Has he been allowed to change? Have you heard from him, talked to him? Aren't there two sides to everything?" He turned slowly.

"You don't understand," I said hotly. "You don't know how long this has been happening: since I was a kid. He is my father, remember, You think I like this. Even Kamal agrees that a divorce is the best thing. Wife abusers can't change—don't change."

"People have changed. People change. The scope for change is unlimited and infinite!" He came and sat next to me.

"All the facts and statistics show they don't . . . I've got it all there on my desk."

"Aha! Is this about your mother and father or about men and women?" He looked amused. This was a game for him.

"They are inseparable . . . "

"Valmiki—the great Indian saint who first composed the *Ramayan*, in Sanskrit—is an extraordinary example. He was a highwayman and a murderer. He became one of the most respected men—a saint in his own lifetime and there are other examples . . . "

"Myth, stories, a different time, a different thing. You can't argue with the statistics . . . "

"Whose statistics? In which society, dealing with what kinds of cultures and people? And do the compilers set out to document the instances of men who have been batterers and have changed? Statisticians are as biased as anyone else. There is nothing like empirical science and figures . . . "

"That is what you men say when you are not using the statistics."

"Is this going to happen all the time now?" He asked quietly.

"What?" I asked aggressively.

"Is our marriage going to be a testing ground for feminism?"

"If necessary."

"I see," he said getting up, "Feminism!"

"Is it a dirty thing? What do you know of it? You said once that you can't dismiss a thing unless you know!"

"To me, yes. As dirty as communism or capitalism. And what is love? Does any condition, any *ism* have any place for love? If your feminism is something which says women should not depend on men for anything but network among women i.e. don't depend on men but *depend* on women, as in the brochure from the Ontario Women's Bureau, then I have absolutely no use for such a feminism . . . and let us not argue about this too. Do what you have to do . . . "

"I told you before don't go messing around with my things."

"What is the big deal about a *public* brochure?"

He walked away. But I was furious he had read the brochure on my desk.

We had already had an argument about privacy before. I had come in late one night from classes, because I had misplaced my car keys and had to go back to look for them. "So?" he asked then as I took off my coat. "Listen," I told him, "when you go out and stay late I don't question you. I also have a right to privacy. You have to trust me. If I want to tell you I will. Don't question me. Let me tell you in my time!"

Our short, brief happiness after my return from that first trip to New York ended. He became less talkative. Occasionally he came in very late. He would just go out and say he would be late, and that was all. I felt that he was baiting me for a quarrel so I did not mention his late nights. It was near the June month end when Ma called again. Pa had got notice that she was filing for a divorce and had gotten drunk and came hammering on her door. She had to call the cops who came and arrested him. Dookie was sitting next to me and he must have figured out from the scraps of our conversation what had happened. Ma was crying and I was trying to calm her.

"Next weekend is a holiday weekend, why don't you go," Dookie said suddenly. Ma was still on the phone. "Right now she needs somebody," he added. It was what I was thinking and I felt a spurt of gratitude for him. It was as though he were reading my mind.

"When you go, perhaps you can see if she can get some time off and come back with you. Some time away from it all might help her . . ." He called the airline, made reservations for me and was so supportive, I forgive him his hangups about feminism.

That trip we did go away to Jersey City and coming back at night, Kamal drove over the Verrazanno bridge. It was more beautiful than I imagined. Kamal had suggested that Ma move to another apartment, but Ma was reluctant. She was close to work and right on the subway. All the tenants knew her and the area was bright and busy. She felt safe there. When She took me around I felt that she was right. And why should she run away? She was not the culprit, she was not a criminal—if anyone was, it was Pa. Ma was feeling better and I was glad I visited her. I also needed the break from my work and the tension between Dookie and myself.

When I returned to Toronto Dookie was as happy as I had not seen him since I had returned from New York City after my first trip. It was infectious. I felt happy too and when we entered our apartment, the sunshine streaming through the windows made the apartment look crisp and bright. I knew then that it was because Ma's apartment was dull and grubby-looking, even the pavements in her area and the streets somehow looked grubby, though there was a vitality about New York I liked. I settled back quickly into my routine of work, classes, studies and speaking almost weekly with Ma. Dookie started going out more often by himself and at first I was glad, but he came in late and this started to nag at me, especially as he was very vague about what he was doing. One night, I put on the night latch and when he came in at two a.m. he could not get in. I got up and opened the door.

"Pretty late," I said. His silence was irritating. "So?" I asked.

"So what?"

"What's the story tonight?"

"No story," he said casually ignoring me and heading for the bedroom. "And why are you questioning me? You were the one who said that we should trust each other. You were the one who said that I must not question you about your whereabouts! Why are you questioning me about mine? And anyway what does it matter? We have a poor excuse for a marriage—and don't give me that crap about new values in the family and your feminist theories!"

"Then maybe we should go our separate ways," I added. It had always worked in the past. At the slightest mention of separation he would stop, take stock and come up with a hundred ways why we should stay together, why our marriage could work. He said nothing and changed into his pyjamas and went to his side of the bed. I joined him quietly. When the alarm went and I opened my eyes his arm was around me and I cuddled up to him. We ignored the alarm and later when we finally got up, we both called in sick. We had never done that before.

"I am researching the nightlife of Toronto for a book—my research is almost through. I've already started my book," he said during lunch at the Olive Garden.

"Sure?" I teased.

"Not quite," he laughed.

"Talking about writing—that's what we're doing in this course. Women writers!" I added, "I never realized how biased society was as regards women and writing until now." I was unable to stop myself.

Dookie just laughed, "Some of the greatest poetry of India was written by Indian women—going as far back as the first century AD— numerous poems in the *Sattasai* were believed composed by women but unfortunately the information is sketchy. I have heard some women critics cite that as an example of the male bias."

"Well isn't it?" I asked, doing my best to sound casual.

"No. Those same critics—women and some men—fail to see the overall picture. The same lack of information applies to all the male poets in the very anthology. It was not a deliberate singling out of women, and if it was, then all that Hala, the compiler of the anthology, had to do was delete all gender references and those women poets would have been completely invisible, lost for all practical purposes of gender cognition. That was so easy to do! But then you have to understand the context of the culture of the time: to take a 'modern' —read eurocentric—critique or value system and apply it to a certain place and time is more than faulty. The fact is that in Indian literature there are no known authors for a large body of work for a number of reasons—one of the most important being that many of the composers were poet-saints and the closer they got to selfhood, the more they realized that they did not own anything, the more they realized that all expression, poetry, painting the 'arts' are manifestations of the ego. So they wrote, deliberately deleting themselves from the work, uncon- cerned about being credited for a work of art . . . Nothing to do with gender . . . "

"I've heard this before," I taunted him. I had not and I did not even realize that he was as conscious about women writers.

"You know all these *isms* are a failure when interpreting certain cultures and times and places, or when stacked against the science of the soul . . . but let's leave all this ritual and chanting and telling of the beads and *isms*—outside there is sunshine, a thousand shades of green, birds on limbs, on branches where we left our hearts to dry in the sun—remember the crocodile who liked monkey-heart-soup?" We spent much of the afternoon in Sunnybrook Park and I had forgotten how such simple things could be so fulfilling. We had entered one of those times when nothing we said to each other could be offensive.

"So are we going to start a family?" We were walking back to the car.

"Yes," I said, 'but not now—I want to finish my degree first."

"Yes. You're right. And I have my masterpiece to write." He pulled in his breath and pushed out his chest in mock seriousness. I think we were still laughing when we got to our apartment. There was a subtle change. Though he stayed out late occasionally, he went out less frequently. He spent more time at home, at his desk writing, reading and staring out the window. He scribbled furiously and there seemed to be an urgency in all his activities. His muse had taken possession of him. He was obsessed with his scribbling and I was glad. Somehow I seemed to draw a strength of purpose from his motivation and I felt more relaxed.

When I got my vacation in August and September he changed his mind about going to New York with me. I was not disappointed. I felt that he was on to something important, novel and new and he could not break off, did not want to break off.

"You know, the soul is genderless," he said very pensively as he drove me to the airport, "colourless, the body is merely a manifestation of a particular mind-soul lost in desires and misdeeds. A tightrope of accrued karma and the desire, sometimes strong, sometimes weak, to burn out that karma, pay back those we are indebted to—even in such an ego-extension thing as fiction or 'art.' Shah Jahan built the Taj, Bronte a Rochester and I a not-I . . . I threw all my manuscripts away yesterday."

"What, where?" I was shocked.

"When I went down to the lakeshore . . . "

"Why, why . . . ?"

"O, I need to start over. It wasn't going well. Writers do that all the time!" He laughed at himself, inhaling and pushing out his chest. We laughed together.

*

Ma is excited now that I am here in New York City. The divorce finally came through and a Kashmiri Moslem man is interested in her. I wonder at his interest in Ma, and if he is another of the thousands of illegal aliens in New York seeking any means for acquiring American citizenship. Perhaps I have read too much about the Moslem militants in Kashmir, the fatwah on Rushdie's head, imbibed some of Dookie's distaste for Islam—maybe a little of all. Well, my nani was an unwilling convert from Hinduism to Islam, and so too in all probability were my people going back five hundred or a thousand years. Who knows? Here from the roof of Ma's lowrise apartment building there is the Manhattan skyline in the distance, sticking up in the dusk sun like grass stalks from the liquidy gold of another sunset on the overflowing conservancy, on the savannah of our childhood village of another place and time.

"Shaira," Dookie said this afternoon on the phone from Toronto, "I'm glad you have your mother there. Well . . . " he had paused, "well, I've moved out. I have filed for a divorce. It couldn't work. It's time for me to start a family now. I am growing old. I can't wait and our marriage has become the testing-ground for your feminism! I'm tired of fighting, life's too short for fighting. The only fight I was ever interested in, we left behind. That's why we ran away to Canada, remember? It'll be half and half—all we have. The details we can look at later. Perhaps we'll talk later. Well—goodbye."

Memory can be dredged up from the past, created, recreated, recalled and invented but that reverses nothing. Still, I wonder how things would have turned out if Ma had agreed to the marriage . . .

"Shaira?" Ma calls softly even before her head appears from behind the stairwell door leading to the roof of this grubby lowrise apartment building.

"Here."

"You got a call just now?"

"Yes."

"Was it Kamal . . . ?" She stops midway. Perhaps she knows.

"Dookie. Just Dookie—perhaps I will write him, one day soon . . . yes, he would disagree with Soyinka . . . "

"Who?"

"An African writer—never mind. Ma, isn't the sunset over Manhattan beautiful?"

"Yes."

We stare in silence. A car horn blares below. Someone else tramps noisily up the stairwell. We are one, two then three—and one again.

Part Two

S T Writerji

Those of us who are writers, unsuccessful writers, commercially unsuccessful writers are always writing masterpieces. Our most recently
completed manuscripts or our works-in-progress are the manuscripts
which would take us from obscurity to fortune and fame yet somehow,
once our project is over, this never quite happens. And it is always a
question of the right publisher. This does not necessarily mean we are
unhappy writers. We are after all, the brahmins of the literary world!
We write, we often tell ourselves, not for the money, nor even the fame
but because we have to, because we were born into the caste of the
writer. Am I fooling myself . . . ?

You would not be surprised to hear that my name is S T Writerji. It
is funny how they gave me this name! Having lived all their lives in
the west my parents settled for very western names, hoping that I
would fit in and not be dogged by an alien-sounding name, so they
called me Soon Tomorrow. What a euphemism for hope and triumph,
they thought! As you can guess, all through school, college and university Soon Tomorrow became synonyms for the perpetual loser and
so I shortened it to just S T. There was no way I could escape the "ji"
after "Writer" and I have often been forced to explain that "ji" is an
Indian-language suffix signifying respect as in Gandhi—Gandhi-ji.

I don't know how it happened but one thing led to another and I realized that I must be a writer. You may say that it was bound to happen, the karma of my name. It is a complicated business, this naming bit. The pandits opened a book, never mind what they called it, and looked at the time, the movement and position of stars, they made complex mathematical calculations—at least my parents felt they did—and the name arrived, a badge announcing my most dominant trait. Soon Tomorrow! So I wrote this masterpiece, just wrote it and began sending out queries to all sorts of publishers and anticipating the mailman everyday.

No easy thing, mind you! I have been published before and you would think that that would make it easier. Not so. My publisher, a gentleman and a great soul lives in California, was born there. Something about the air there brings out the goodness in people and some people believe that it is some sort of spiritual centre of the planet Earth as say Jerusalem or Varanasi are. Have you noticed how all these swamis and yogis come from India and set up their ashrams there, generate huge gatherings and set up branches later in all parts of North America and Europe? Yogananda set up his headquarters there. He and his yoga were big things in the 1920s and right through until he left his body in 1952. Chai, my publisher, had found out long ago that even Elvis Presley read Yogananda—the purity of California by the sea! These days Pandit Ravi Shanker makes his home there—perhaps India has lost its holiness and soul! I understand that Dr Deepak Chopra is going to set up some institute on Alternative Medicine—Ayurvedic Medicine—there in California near the sea! Even Hollywood finds the air pure! So my publisher Chai Bhai, whose grandfather served in the Scottish Highland regiment in India, while doing his doctoral thesis suddenly came upon Naipaul's *The Mimic Men* and decided that he would do his thesis on the Indian writers of the Caribbean. He heard so many stories of India from his grandfather who had moved to California after he had retired from the British army that he felt like a diaspora Indian himself. An Angrezi babu!

He had heard that Elvis thing and wanted to reciprocate! Peter Jennings had just interviewed a guy called Peter Nazareth on ABC's

World News Tonight. Peter Nazareth had just come out of the bush, so to speak, out of Africa, and started teaching Elvis 101. The first university course on Elvis. I mean, many people idolized Elvis but to make him serious stuff in university, never mind it was a university in a third-world state like Iowa, was real way-out stuff. The media all went to see and talk to Nazareth until he mentioned the Cherokee thing, that Elvis's great-great-grandmother was Cherokee, and that his maternal grandmother was Jewish, that there was Scots-Irish blood too on the other side, that Elvis was a great champion for repressed peoples all over the world—Blacks, Native Americans, Hawaiians, Indians . . . Nazareth and his class started showing how Elvis was a great assimilator of Black culture, Cherokee culture, Indian culture, all sorts of cultures and how he paid them back in his songs, costumes and movies! The great white, red-necked god, The king of rock 'n' roll, a channel for world culture suddenly revealed in "a brown mantle"! He was tainted! Elvis the Pelvis was really Elvis the Cherokee! The Jew could come later!

The media quickly dropped him. Chai Bhai felt that had Nazareth been a white American, all might have been well for him, but Nazareth came from Uganda, at a time when Idi Amin the General was up and expelled all the Indians from the country.

But Chai Bhai was prompted to dig up his own family tree. He had heard a rumour that his own great-grandfather, who had served in India during the 1857 Indian war of independence, had married a deposed Indian maharani.

It was the Elvis thing! Elvis's Indian looks and his Cherokee ancestor. And Chai Bhai found out that his own great-grandmother was Indian—from India! Until then he had thought of himself as this great white American reading one of these little colonial boys trying their hands at the master language. He had started reading Naipaul's *The Mimic Men* flippantly, just to please a girl called Rita who had passed herself off as Mexican. She had come into the States via the Rio Grande but was actually an Indian from Trinidad. The oil boom was over, Sir Dr Eric Williams, the charismatic Trinidad prime minister and distinguished historian was dead, the oil money was all gone and Blacks were turning on Indians! Trinidad is a tiny island so she fled. Rita who was babysitting for Chai's wife was reading *The Mimic Men.* Chai never told me he was fucking her and she dared him to read the work of a "great writer." Well he did and made a switch to the Indian writers of the Caribbean—Naipaul, Ismith Khan and Sam Selvon, all from the tiny island of Trinidad—for his doctoral thesis, showing how they carried India in their works. Chai found out too that one of Selvon's great-grandmother was half Scottish and half Indian. When he found out how the Indians of Guyana were discriminated against so that with a larger Indian population than Trinidad they could not produce a single Indian writer of note, he decided to start a publishing house to give them voice, and their works and lives the validity they had lost in the Kennedy years.

Kennedy was not only busy "bedding the blonde." It was after the Cuban missile crisis. Castro was entrenched and Jagan, "the Communist" had won another British Guiana election and that was untenable. With British and American help his opponents burned Georgetown to the ground and destabilized the "Indian-Communist" Jagan government. I was young then, but I remember the British soldiers in full battle dress, the racial tension between Blacks and Indians and my father's snapshots of Water Street and Regent Street in flames. We fled to America when dead men voted for Burnham and he won the title of Kabaka.

I became a writer of sorts. Chai Bhai found me in New York and published my novel. Was I glad for the recognition! When he published another book *Canada Geese and Apple Chatney*—stories of illegal West Indians in the Big Apple, I thought I was on my way to being made. It was only a matter of time I felt, but I never saw a statement from Chai Bhai's Cobra House or received a cent. It didn't matter. I was the brahmin of the literary world! I didn't write for money and besides I would win a prize, some prize that Chai Bhai never entered my books for. I would be reviewed by some journal or newspaper that Chai Bhai never sent my books to, I would be read by some student in some library that never saw a catalogue from Cobra House . . . Chai got grants and published more and yet more books by diaspora Indians, storing them in his basement instead of marketing them. He was signing contracts and tying writers down for five to ten years before publishing them. It was hard to tell when the Scotsman was working but he was a superb editor. And he had a heart of silver, a soul of Gold, a voice of pure sugar-cane juice when he explained the difficulties of small-press publishing long distance from California. That California of pure air by the sea, somewhere near Yogananda's ashram. Elvis read Yogananda and so he had to be Jesus-hearted. Yogananda felt the Christ was a great incarnation and somewhere in a San Diego valley Christ and Krishna walked hand in hand. Chai read Yogananda.

I had thought that any writer who received a response to a query letter from a major publisher should get published. Kerouc wrote on the road. I was writing off the road, inside, about the ashrams in the pure air of California, and you would believe an American publisher would be interested. Well, as Chai said, Nazareth not being a white American and teaching Elvis 101 was not quite right. And it was not quite right for another Indian to write about Indian ashrams or Indian philosophy in America. Kerouac was alright. He was not Indian. I didn't believe Chai about the white thing in the excitement of the response from Farrar, Farrar & Farrar. Palaffsi said, "Send sample chapters!" When he finally replied he said, "I admire the care you have taken with the manuscript but . . ." he had read only two chapters. DoubleDoom said, "An intriguing and complex novel—cut out the political musings on racist America." I cut the "political musings" amounting to one hundred and fourteen pages and toned down the colour obsessions and sent it back. They said after a month, "We admire the care you have taken with this work. It is now a much better work but . . . it is still too long. We hope you find a suitable publisher." They were bidding on Seth's thousand-page novel. A month just to check the length of the work and to hope I find a suitable publisher!

I have been looking for a suitable publisher for years—even Chai Bhai cut out my important passages on politics! A suitable publisher would enter your books for all awards, make advances which she could not afford, get the books in bookstores, publicize your work, proclaim you a genius . . . I would never cut a line or delete a word—only typos or grammar. I would enter competitions and win the prizes for myself, give myself large advances, call myself names. I would be the most suitable publisher.

But would I publish myself until I write "The Great Novel of the English Language"? Would you? Well, with these "love letters" out of my way, let me return to my masterpiece which I will never give to any but the most suitable publisher. I can be patient now and wait for one of my caste—a brahmin publisher! One had even said from foggy London, "Send me reviews of your previous work that would make me want to change my mind!"

"I wish you luck placing it elsewhere." Did she? Obviously not a brahmini! To remember the strictures: watch the length—long novels don't sell; stories are difficult for a new writer, cut the facts on racism—your audience are after all the very people accused, watch those sexist tendencies of characters—most of the editors at the major houses are women and feminists—a book on the do's and don'ts.

Well, my name is S T Writerji and I am working on my masterpiece man-U-script!

These Ghosts of Ghosts

I had always felt that Raju would be recognized for his writing. Well, you have to understand that I was younger and in that first flush of love when the sky, moon and stars are touchable, when anything is possible. And I believed in him, believed he would be a great and famous poet, that he would be known all over the world—and I for inspiring all his great love poems. But then the others touched us; fingers on the wings of the monarch butterfly, and the colour came away. We grew older very rapidly: that other affair which led to his marriage; I too marrying and coming to New York: a new world, a husband I knew nothing about. Ritesh at the time having just completed his degree in sociology wanted to get married. His mother in New York contacted mine in Guyana through a mutual friend. And so they made the trip to Guyana. We met. He liked what he saw—Raju had just got married and I wanted to put distance between us—and we married. Soon I was in New York; a new place, a new world with the pressures of work and adapting and then the baby.

I had forgotten about Raju, about writers and writing until my husband's cousin Anand turned up unexpectedly at our door one evening. Anand had come into New York from Toronto—illegally. He had no place to stay, a small handbag of clothes and little money. I was furious, not because we couldn't find space for him in our apartment, but because Ritesh seemed to be expecting him, and as they talked after dinner and a few drinks it became clearer that they had had a plan of sorts, had been in communication for some time. Ritesh had said nothing to me and later that night when I asked him, he hid in his "menbusiness" and some "things it best if yuh don't know," which always infuriated me. Anand's refusal to serve National Service in order to graduate at the university back home was news in the West Indian papers here, and while for weeks we followed the case and the political storm it caused, all Ritesh had said in his crisp, inarticulate way at the time was, "My cousin—always the one to speak up as kids." There was an unobtrusive pride in the way he said it.

But Ritesh relented and became a bit more communicative. Anand had had to escape to North America to save his life. Well, who couldn't have guessed that! I was not so long away in New York that I didn't know what it was like back there. Reluctantly, I agreed to put up Anand for as long as we could, but as the weeks went by and I got to know him I was glad that we did. He was very helpful around the house in between his various odd jobs. On weekends when he wasn't working he and Ritesh would do the groceries, or he would take Surin for long walks, to museums or into downtown Manhattan. Surin was three, and he would come home excited about all the things he and "Uncle Anand" had seen and done. Perhaps we liked him because by taking Surin out on weekends he gave Ritesh and me time to ourselves. It was in his fourth month with us that he started to write. At nights when we had finished dinner, he would sit at the kitchen table and scribble bits of poems, and later his novel.

When he left, another six months had gone by, and he had just finished the first draft of his novel. It was a cold Saturday morning in March and we were still asleep when the immigration officers knocked on our door. At eight o'clock on a Saturday morning we all suspected the worse. Anand had time to grab his manuscript and the clothes in the small bag, prepacked for such a contingency, and scramble down the fire escape from the window in his room. Somebody had informed on him. A few years later he would write of a similar incident in his story collection, *Canada Geese and Apple Chatney*—and we all laughed reading it. He even suggested in his story that the officers were kind people and had come at that hour so that all were forewarned and had time to escape: theirs a futile job. There is no cure. Everyone knows that one in ten persons in New York City is an illegal alien. At the time there was no laughter. Anand was in his pyjamas, and without shoes or coat and had taken temporary refuge in the garbage room, hiding under bags of garbage.

From the time Anand starting scribbling I began to recall Raju. Six years in New York had zipped by and I was beginning to feel that I had lived here all my life—Guyana like some distant dream. But with Anand's arrival and his writing, Guyana became a dream filled with Raju, and I regretted then that I had burnt all those love poems he wrote me.

*

It must have been the day after I went to see him that last time. I had thought, previously to that when I saw him—he had just started seeing that girl from the Royal Bank—that it was over between us, though later I felt that perhaps things between them might fizzle out. He had said once that he needed to meet people as a writer, and I had said that I would understand. Perhaps he was testing me, perhaps she was one of those.

That last time . . .

We came out of the Customs Boathouse office, standing close to each other and looking out over the river. It was a clear morning and we were in the shade with the sun behind us. In the distance on the west bank, the ferry was just pulling into the stelling.

"Remember the ferry? The stelling?" I asked. It came out funny because I wanted to laugh at his discomfort.

I had gone to see him inside the Customs Boathouse, and all he'd said so far was, "Let's go outside." It was noisy, busy and unprivate in his office. He had been giving another officer a document when he turned and saw me entering the public doorway and seemed uncertain what to do. The smooth fluent talker silent, trying to collect himself. I was sure he was still in love with me.

"Yes the ferry," He said slowly turning to me. "I'm sorry. You have heard?" He touched the ring on his finger.

"Yes. But is it true?" It could have been a rumour. He could never lie to me so I had to ask him, hear it from him. Nobody had seen an invitation and nobody I knew had witnessed the wedding, not even his best friends. I had felt that he might have been playing a prank, doing this to get me to marry Ritesh. He had known about the offer from Ritesh's parents—and I had teased him about it a few times. Once he had said that I should consider that offer. There was nothing in Guyana for me and there was no place else he wanted to live. And in Guyana there was nothing he could offer me but hope—he hated America.

"Yes. A small, quiet wedding—just her home circle and mine. That was what she wanted."

"Well congratulations. I wish you both a happy life." I was sad and yet relieved. It had happened and there was no turning back. I could go on with my life. We could still love each other but we would not let that affect our marriages.

"Thanks. That means a lot to me," he said and turned away to the river. "Ah yes the ferry!"

We turned to the river and the ferry tied to the stelling on the other bank. "Can I ever forget?" I asked without any bitterness.

"We would hold hands on the deserted bow. Those are some of the best moments of my life. The sun setting on the river rushing out to the Atlantic, red in the evening glow."

"Sindhur you said . . . "

"Yes Devi. I had said Sindhur. I had said, I had said, when we got married I would take this Sindhur from the river and the ocean and bring it to the maroo, offer it to you, make the sacred mark up the middle of your head. And you had teased me about this man your parents wanted to fix you up with in New York. And I had said that if you agreed to marry him I would interrupt your wedding. And if you got married and I didn't know, I would find your house and stand outside until you came out to me—with a placard, saying I loved you only . . ." He turned and smiled, "I still do."

"I know, but you shouldn't say so now," I smiled through the blurred vision. "What happened?"

"It was a rough time for her. I thought we would just be casual friends but the more I learnt, the more I got sucked in. Her parents fighting at home. A brother drinking too much. A sister, pregnant and unmarried—the boyfriend promising to send for her from Toronto but nothing. More quarrels in the home. Well she leant on me—and I couldn't just walk away. I thought I would give her reasons to live, show her the joy of living, the blessing it was to have human form instead of a dog's or a donkey's. Instead, I became her reason to live, her hope. It was difficult to leave, disillusion her. I was scared she would do something to herself if I did . . ."

"And me?"

"You are not like her. You are strong—that's why we have never gone to bed. And I admire and love you for this. It was after we met that last time and you had learnt that I was seeing her—and you said it was over between us . . . I wasn't certain how you would react when you learnt."

"No. I wouldn't picket your house—and send you postcards!" I couldn't help the ironic teasing: we were friends again—talking about our future, only separately this time.

"Thank you," he said. We looked out across the river in the silence. The ferry was moving, gulls flying around it. Higher overhead, swallows sailed in the wind. There was a stillness on the water. The tide was about to turn out. A large ship, low in the water was almost out of the mouth of the Demerara river into the Atlantic ocean. I listened to the water softly clucking on the greenheart wharf pilings below us. A wren called out somewhere in the rafters. A joyous sweet-sad song. And we turned almost in the same moment to each other and laughed. He inched closer. There was a dusk-sad magic in the air which we had known before. I had wanted him to hold me, put his arms around me once more. He didn't.

"They are as beautiful as ever," he said looking down at my toes. In the uncrowded stelling, on the ferry he would stoop quickly and touch my toes when I wore sandals. It was puja, the touch electrifying our bodies. It was always the right time; nothing more meaningful for us. "Devi," he would say, "my goddess, give me your blessing and your love."

"You never told me you met my mother and father at his office. Pa mentioned it a few days ago. And you asked to marry me! Why didn't you ever tell me?"

"Is this why you came?"

"In a way." I felt I owed him something. I felt justified in loving him, especially as at first Ma had always cuttingly said that he only wanted to use me—that he a was a "town bai" and that was what "town bais" always wanted to do. "It was a wonderful thing to do—if you had told me . . . "

"Well they refused so it was no use mentioning it to you. And you refused to run away with me. I didn't really want you to run away because I knew what it meant to you to have your parents' blessings. Everything would have been different you know."

"One thing I never told you about my parents—they eloped and got married because my mother's parents had refused my father. I didn't want to do the same thing . . ."

"I'm sorry," he said, "if I knew. You should have told me . . ." he looked out to the river. If he knew when he met my parents, perhaps it would have made a difference. If he had told me he was going to meet them . . .? Waiting for my bus, he would occasionally stop speaking abruptly and put his fingers to my lips and halt our conversation, "wren," he would whisper, "wind" he would whisper, "waves" and we listened to the sounds magnified in our focused silence.

I put my hand on his forearm—touching him without thinking—and we watched the ferry, still small in midriver, coming towards us.

"The play of karma," I whispered.

"You should get rid of those poems. You don't want them falling into your husband's hands—you're going to marry that guy from New

York?"

"I think so. There is no sense waiting around any more, is there?" Part of me still hoped that there could be some hope, but he said nothing. "I'll tell Ma tonight. Yes you're right about those poems. I would love to keep them. You know what they meant to me. All through those rough months when my mother said all those nasty things, those poems sustained me. At nights when they were all abed I would take them out and read them, feel you next to me, hear you quote those lines, 'Nothing is forever, and nothing lasts for long. Bear that in mind my friends and rejoice.' Only Radha knew of those poems and I let her read some. She thought they were beautiful!"

"I have rough drafts. Later, whenever, if ever you like I can recreate them for you."

"I'll be a good wife—and you will be a good husband?"

"Yes. I will be a good husband. Our dharma. We never met. We never loved. Your hand is comforting," he looked down at my fingers on his forearm.

"I must go. The ferry. I was not to have been in town today, but I had to see you once more." I had taken time off from work.

"Lunch?"

"I would love to. That and all those places-things we never got to— but not today . . ." I couldn't bring myself to say not ever, I still felt some place, some time when it was right. . .

"I'll walk you to the gate—here this way, we'll use the officers' stair." I was looking at the view sweeping inland to the vast South American interior, the faint outline of the floating bridge across the river, the thin line of forest in the distance beyond as we turned to the non-public stairway. It was like a flash of soul-stirring landscape in a dream. He bent and touched my toes.

"Devi—your blessings for this love, for all the love poems I will one day write." He straightened.

"Yes Raju, my Raj. Yes." You could feel the salt water on the wharf. We walked silently. He was married. He would not hold me.

I held his elbow. "Goodbye, Raju—my Raj." He nodded and

leaned on the gate. He was still leaning on the gate when I looked back and when the ferry turned to the other bank. I had never told him how handsome he looked in his uniform. White shirt-jac, polished gold buttons, the golden officer's braids on his shoulders blurring in the distance with the whitish salt water around him.

*

Anand, still illegal in New York when his novel was accepted had used the non de plume, S T Writerji. But just as his collection of stories was released he had received his green card—a genuine one—under an unannounced amnesty. This made for a triple celebration and much laughter in our house, as I had just given birth again. His collection, despite the controversy, was a success—true-to-life, bitter, embarrassing—but funny.

At the Nine-Day celebration for the baby, Ritesh had asked, "Who better than Anand, than Writerji, since Naipaul?" There was much laughter and applause. I had turned to my baby. Raju, my heart said, Raju is better.

*

"Devi—we having a Diwali concert in Queens," Radha said on the phone a month later. "I have tickets for you. Leave the baby with Ma. I'll come for you and Surin. A surprise. No argument. Yuh too shut away since yuh pregnancy!"

"What surprise?"

"No-no-no. Wait till the concert." She teased, "Our secret."

There were three books, not one, by Raju on the display table in the concert hall. I was stunned and yet I should have expected this. I had heard nothing of these publications before. I was exhilarated: the writer, the brochure said, had "accomplished a difficult task in his narratorial integrity of vision . . . " and few other Caribbean writers had achieved that kind of complexity of vision. I picked up extra copies of the brochure for Ritesh and Anand, the comments on the poetry singing in my head, "highly emotionally charged images which allow

110

a reader from whatever culture entrance into the universal experiences of love and regret." Radha was the only other person who knew he had written me those love poems. And touching those books it was like touching him all over again; like him touching my toes so many places in puja. I reread the poems when Ritesh worked late and the children were asleep. One cries for such love, as I did, reading all those beautiful love poems at the end!

On Anand's next visit I showed him the books and flyer. "What do you think of him?"

Anand laughed. "So-so. He just writing, doesn't know what he's doing."

"Do you know what he's doing?" I was surprised at the swiftness of my response. Anand's dismissal of him irked me. He who had taken such pains to learn things, felt them so deeply and gave so willingly to be dismissed so offhandedly.

"No," Anand said straightening up in his chair.

"Then how do you know that he doesn't know what he's doing?"

"You're good." He laughed.

"What makes a writer Anand?" I asked. He had missed the irony.

"Just the fire in your guts to write. It is a very incestuous business though. Most writers write about themselves, their experience—dilute it in some ways, try to disguise it as fiction. And the better the disguise, the better it is as fiction. What, do you want to write?"

"Maybe," I laughed.

"There's an old saying that every person has a good book inside—and there is only one way to find out—and that is to write."

"I don't know—I can never write about myself," and I teased him, "or about writers writing about themselves." They all laughed with me. Writerji was really Anand catching Canada geese, experimenting with apple, as mango was scarce that winter in Toronto, to make chatney.

In *The Ghost of Bellow's Man* Raju had called himself Raj. If I were his Devi, his goddess, he was my Raj I had always reminded him. Raj and Raju are the same. I was pleased that he had used Raj. If Anand could become S T Writerji it was perfectly fine for Raju to become Raj! By the time I got to *The Ghost of Bellow's Man* last week, a centrespread article on him had appeared in the *Caribbean Daylight,* which I found out only when Anand called.

"Did you see this week's *Daylight*?" he asked.

"No."

"Well go and get it. The most extraordinary piece on any writer from the West Indies yet. We were talking of that only recently. It's as though you are a visionary, as though you know something we don't."

*

"GUYANESE WRITER AND POET LIVING IN CANADA"—the large caption above the photograph, the eyes I knew, that head I had held. It was as though the writer of the article, Odaipaul Singh, had heard me and was responding to Anand:

> ". . . the fact that the author was able to excavate the episode from his subconscious and transform apparent despair into a statement of affirmation is an indication of his genius and skill as a writer, a cultural critic and a visionary . . . where he blazes a new trail, however, and where he is bound to evoke controversies in the literary world, is in his conscious application of traditional Hindu theories of aesthetics and poetics . . . his claim that much, if not all, of Indo-Caribbean literature, including the works of Sam Selvon and V S Naipaul, exhibit consciously or unconsciously evidence and traces of these aesthetic principles . . . our historical and cultural past is not limited to the last 150 years. There is a clear continuity that links us to the cultural heritage of India. We may have changed, but change is not discontinuity. I agree with him when he claims that the worldview that informs his writing is Indic . . . "

Singh himself had done his doctorate on Indian philosophy and was a well-known and often controversial activist in New York. Who else was better placed to make such statements, trace that elusive Indianness we search for?

It had always haunted Raju. Listening to him read Tagore and the Upanishads aloud in the huge, quiet stelling at Vreed-en-hoop as we waited for my bus was like reading from his own soul. The greatest poetry was in the Upanishads—Shakespeare was not half as accomplished over a broader range of genres than Tagore! Raju would give me his books of Upanishadic poetry and reading them I too came to feel as he did.

"Anand. Have you finished reading *Ghost*?" I asked Anand on the phone.

"Yes."

"Question. Why did you think he called the book *The Ghost of Bellow's Man*?"

"It seems to be a clear parody of Saul Bellow's protagonist in his first novel *Dangling Man*. Bellow won the Nobel Prize for literature."

"Could the ghost be anything else?"

"Perhaps, perhaps the Indian doctor, Govinda Lal I think, in *Mr Sammler's Planet* or. . . " his voice rose perceptibly, "or Raju in R K Narayan's *The Guide*. Never thought about it seriously, I just assumed . . . And you?"

"Could it be love? He is rejected all the time even by the publishers—and that really means nothing. Acceptance by the publishers as a substitute for acceptance by people, the woman he loves. He is rejected and moves from one girl, or woman to another. Wasn't Raju in *Guide* rejected by Rosie, the woman he loved? And going away he passed himself off as a holy man, which sort of made up for his past excesses? The fantasies? Well, I don't know because I only saw the film *Guide* which is based on the novel!" Raju and I had seen the film together. He had seen it long ago, not realising then that it was based on the novel by R K Narayan, but had liked it very much. It was a film which haunted me all the way to the stelling and beyond. Raju, sensing this while we sat in the waiting room, started talking about the trick which Narayan had Raju play on himself. "To be a rogue, but to pass oneself off as good, and be forced to play that role of the good, having to live the role to play it convincingly, until it transformed the rogue without the rogue wanting to be transformed."

"Wow—you have been thinking of this thing a lot. It's almost becoming an obsession! Set it down, set it all down!"

I laughed. Perhaps Anand would get it. It would be safe with him—he was after all Writerji. But they all missed it, and it was so clear. The essence of Chapter Five through to the end of the chapter, the essence of the novel; this girl who might be me, that girl I probably once was.

And am I now the ghost of Bellow's man—Bellow's woman? Writing that one book we all have inside? You wonder what he would think when he hears of these stories, of these ghosts of the ghost of Bellow's man roaming! Well no—let him come! Ah, to see his face again; soon, soon. These ghosts of ghosts we never get rid of—even when we walk in light!

Canada Geese and Apple Chatney

Bai dhem time something else—rough—rough like rass. And was no laughter. Yuh want hear about dhem time? Leh me tell yuh. And don't bother with Writerji. He's mih friend but remember he's a writer. He change-up everything, mix-up people and place so nobady could tell who is who, and what what. And if yuh ain't know, all sound like true. But dhat is because Writerji good. Well he always good. Yuh see dhat story about running from immigration officer which set in New York. Dhat same thing happen here in Toronto to he. And was he, me and Hermit sharing a apartment at the same time. Yuh know how Anand get dhat name Writerji? Is me give he, me and Hermit. Ask Hermit when yuh see he.

And dhat bai Hermit is something else. A holiday—was Christmas. Just the three ah we in the apartment. Snow like ass outside. Prem and Kishore invite we over but Hermit old car ain't starting, and anyway too much snow. And Prem and Kishore ain't gat car—dhey living in the east end, somewhere behind gaad back near Morningside. In dhem days, once people know yuh illegal, nobady want see yuh, nobady invite yuh at them house. Even yuh own relative—people come hey and change. Money, money, money. Mih own uncle don't call me. And when he ass going to UG he staying at we place, five years—mih mother neva tek a cent from he. When yuh illegal everybody think yuh

115

want money, or something. Yuh don't let people know you situation—
yuh laugh outside. So is just dhe three a we. Snow tearing tail and we
putting lash on some Johnnie Walker black label. Hermit bring out he
big tape and we playing some Mukesh and Rafi. Suddenly the tape
finish. Is a eerie silence. Fat snow flakes khat khat khat on dhe window pane.

Suddenly Hermit seh, "And Writerji—a hope yuh ain't turn out like
Naipaul. Yuh see how he write *Miguel Street* and *Biswas*. Mek a
mockery a everybody, mek a mockery a dhe culture. . ."

"Ah come on Hermit. Naipaul nat so bad. He write fiction, stories.
And stories are more than just the truth, more than just a little lie. And
we more critical than Naipaul. Remember how we say dhat all pandit
ah bandit! What more derogatory than that."

"But we say it as joke!"

"Same thing with Naipaul!"

"Anyway, Mek sure yuh ass don't write nothing about me."

"He gat to write about something Hermit," I teasing Hermit, "and
what you gun do if he write about you?" Since Guyana we calling he
Hermit because he like a bookworm, always reading when yuh miss
he. Was dhe same thing here. When he come home and after he eat,
he head straight fuh he room and read. Sometimes he look TV with we.

"Well we friends a lang time, since high school but don't do dhis to
me. I serious. Don't let me recognize anything about me." Man is like
dhe cold come inside the apartment. Hermit serious real serious. Rare
thing for Hermit. Since I come to Toronto only one time I see he so
serious and angry. I tell you, dhem quiet people, yuh could neva tell.
Funny how we always teasing he about he hook nose and he long hair
since school days. Anybady with a joke about finding anything, is
Hermit nose could find it. Anybady want string to tie anything, is Hermit hair. Talk about bird, is description by length and curve of beak—
like Hermit beak-nose. When yuh can't find anybady—dhey gaan into
seclusion like Hermit. But Hermit always laugh. Dhis time Hermit serious.

That other time was a month or two before. We gaan up Jane Street to see Hetram but Hetram ain't home yet. So Hermit seh let we say go across to the Jane-Finch mall at dhe McDonalds. Buy coffee and some chicken burger or something—he paying—and check out the girls. Funny thing about Hermit was he like spend a lat a time by heself but when he come outside is like he can't get enough of people, place, things. And he pleasant and outgoing. If a nice chick pass, Hermit lose shyness. He gan straight up to she and tell she she nice, sometimes mek a date with she or something. Was a Sunday and dhe mall full because of the flea market. McDonald's full to. So Writerji and me go and hold a table while Hermit in the line. Me and Writerji surveying everybady else. Suddenly a little commotion start up before the cashier. Hermit and a dread squaring off. Me and Writerji run up.

"Listen man. I'm in this line before you. Yuh just want to come from nowhere and get infront me!" Hermit voice not loud but like a spring, one hand in he jacket pocket. Well yuh know Jane-Finch area. Plenty West Indians, plenty Jamaicans with dhey drugs and crime and bullying people like dhey own dhe whole place. We think Hermit holding he wallet because of pickpocket.

"Listen —I gettin serve now coolie bai."

"Not before me *rass*-ta." Hermit deliberately breaking up the word. The dread black like tar and about four inches taller than Hermit, long dreadlocks and one a dhem green and red cap with Selassie picture. Hermit about 5' 9", not exactly short, he hair long like a yogi, and he skin fair. A odd contrast and similarity.

"I gettin serve now or is shooting."

"Not before me *rass*-ta." Hermit turning squarely to dhe dread and straightening and suddenly smiling, "friend I is a peaceful man—like Gandhi—you know Gandhi. Believe in nonviolence. But lil advice from me; when yuh talk about shooting yuh should gat a gun in yuh hand first. I know people—nat me— who would shoot yuh dhe moment yuh talk about shooting. I know people—nat me—who would shoot yuh cunt dead, now, if yuh talk another word." I getting cold-sweat hearing Hermit. He ain't afraid though he smiling. And I thinking, praying that the dread and he partner ain't start shooting fuh truth.

I think we dead. Well is Jane-Finch mall and a whole crowd a Jamaicans suddenly stan up behind dhe dread. Just Hermit and me and Writerji near he. Dhem Indians and white people stay right at dhem table like sheep. Everything happening like lightning.

"Next cashier open here," a supervisor said smiling and breaking the tension. "May I help you here sir," she said pleasantly. She just open a cashier near the dread. Nothing like a pretty white girl to disarm a dread! Dread turn to she with a swagger and smiling like Hermit ain't exist. Later when we in the car driving home Writerji burst out, "Hermit I think we dead man. Nearly piss mih pants."

"Nah. He just bluffing."

"What if he tek out a gun?" I ask.

"If he only put he hand in he coat pocket. I woulda shoot dhe bitch. An he know it."

"With what?"

"This." Hermit reach into he jacket and tek out a small blue automatic gun.

"Yuh mean yuh holding that thing all dhe time? How lang yuh gat this man!" Writerji tek the gun and examine it fine fine.

"When I first come to this country." Man I in shock. I live with Hermit for six months and neva know this. But Hermit in Canada six years before me. And he live in Montreal most a dhe time. Same time I come from Georgetown, same time he come down from Montreal. Dhem Frenchie racial he seh and dhem want dhem own country. Like if dhem own anything. Is thief they thief dhe land from dhem Amerindians—and don't matter Frenchie lose dhe 1980 referendum. Next time round and next time. Toronto tame compared to Montreal . . .

Well me and Writerji remember this incident and the gun same time, and how Hermit cool like cucumber and scared a nobody. Suddenly Writerji smile. "Hermit—relax my friend. Ah know yuh hungry. Well this meat defrost. I will cook some—curry?"

"Nah how about some bunjal geese," Hermit laughed, "and a bake one—come, I'll come and help you. Put on dhat Sundar-Popo tape

Jones." Hermit turn to me a bit unsteady. He nicknamed me Jones because I see Jim Jones when he first land in Guyana, and because I went and see he fraud miracle in Sacred Heart Church lang before all them murders. Well I start one big laugh. And Hermit start laughing too.

I tell yuh, times was tough. Hermit just come down from Montreal—he just get he landed and want make a new start—he give too many false name and false social insurance number in Montreal, and dhem Frenchie getting more racial—I coming up from GT and illegal, then baps, Writerji landing down on we. See how things happen! Remember dhem time when government thugs try to break up we meeting at Kitty Market Square and dhey get beat up and run in the police station for help. Was me, Cuffy and Akkara and some other bais from Buxton. They shoot Akkara in dhe gardens and seh he had gun fuh overthrow deh government, and dhey beat up Cuffy in he garage and put a AK-47 in he car trunk and seh he about to resist arrest, that he commit suicide in jail. All this just after Rodney assassination. Well I ain't wait around. Them days yuh didn't had to get visa to come to Canada. Next flight I in Toronto. But mih uncle and he wife meking all sort a remark. If I bathe two times a day—that was a summer hotter than anything in Guyana—they complaining I bathe too lang and too often, I go to the toilet too often—is money water cost. This nat Guyana! Yuh pay fuh water here! Well a meet Hermit in Knob Hills Farm one day and he seh he gat same prablem, he went through same thing—leh we rent a two bedroom. I ain't gat no wuk yet you know. He seh man no prablem. He get a social insurance number and a name fuh mih. Some Indian name. The man dead and one a Hermit girlfriend get the name and number. Frank Sharma. See how Frank stick. All yuh must be think that I change mih name, become Frank instead of Ramesh because I want become Canadian duck. Nah. This coolie ain't shame he name. Anyway I Frank Sharma now. And frighten like ass when I go any place to wuk and I gat to say I name Frank Sharma. I trembling but trying to look bold, hoping I ain't say meh real name.

Yuh think is three cents we go though! Well I ain't gat no wuk yet and Hermit just pick up a thing in a factory. Although he just get he landed, money still small. Almost a month and I ain't get nothing, then I walk in a factory at Steeles and Bathurst desperate—and get tek on. The supervisor want a forklift operator. Man I neva drive a donkey-cart yet muchless forklift. I tell the man, with experience, I could manage dhe forklift, anything. Lucky for me the forklift break down, and the forklift driver who didn't show up, turn up next day. The supervisor find wuk for me packing boxes. And next two weeks bam, Writerji turn up in the apartment lobby. He dhe last man to land in Canada before Canadian immigration decide yuh gat to get visa from Guyana, too much Guyanese fulling up Toronto. We bunking on dhe ground, can't afford a bed or even mattress, in a room and squeezing cents. Hermit trying to get a name and number for Writerji.

Well, Writerji waiting fuh he name and number but he ain't wasting time. He want learn about Toronto and Canada. He find library and reading up about Canada, about trees and birds. Whenever we go out anyway he pointing out birch, spruce, oak, cedar, weeping willow, pussy willow, ash, he pointing out bluejay, redstart, sparrow, starling, cardinal. He teking walk in park—yuh want know which park? Is at Eglinton and Jane street—Eglinton Flats. Autumn coming and Writerji want experience Canadian fall—colours radiant over all dhem trees. Geese coming in to land sweet sweet like plane. Every afternoon he coming home and writing poems. A night he writing a poem and suddenly he buss out one big laugh. He seh we thinking money scarce and cutting we tail and food all over dhe place. All them geese nice and fat, heading south fuh winter. He seh if is Guyana yuh think all them duck could deh so nice and lazy all over dhe place, preening themself like majesty and nobady own them, and people starving? And other people feeding them bread and fattening them up fuh we!

He seh why we don't catch some a dhem geese and stock up for winter. Them geese heading south to get away from the cold and now is dhe right time. And he tell we how in England dhem bai do dhe same thing and some Trini writer name Selvon write about this thing in a book call *Lonely Londoners*. Hermit remember he hear this some-way but he laugh and seh nobady neva write this— and how he know? Tell yuh the truth, I see them geese and I thinking same thing —how dhem bais in Guyana woulda done wuk them down.

"Is how I know? I'm a writer man!"

"So Hermit is Gandhi like Gandhiji and yuh is Writer —like Writ-erji," I buss out one laugh.

Well Hermit still ain't believe that this thing write down so Writerji and we gone to St Dennis library near Weston Road and Eglinton corner and he get Hermit to borrow *The Lonely Londoners* and *Ways of Sunlight* by Sam Selvon. As soon as we get home he find the page and start read how hunger washing Cap tail and Cap decided to ketch sea-gull and eat them. We laugh good. And dhat is how he get name dhe Writerji. From dhat night we call he Writerji. But he done plan this thing. We could buy expire bread, and night time head down to Eglin-ton Flats Park. Them Geese sleeping right next to a little culvert and all over the grass behind them trees. Two a-we could catch ducks and one man swipe dhe neck. Hermit get excited. He want try this thing. Well is me and Hermit end up catching all them ducks and geese. I holding them and Hermit swiping them neck. All Writerji doing is holding bag and keeping lookout. Just like he since schooldays. He always thinking up something and me and Hermit doing the wuk. A trunk full a ducks in large double garbage bags. We skin them when we get home. Writerji saying we ain't stupid like Cap and we dispose of them feathers and skin real good. Nobody could catch we. Well them geese taste good.

Hermit seh next weekend let we take some fuh Prem and Kishore. They apartment overlooking Morningside park and them maple trees flaming with colours. Writerji want tek a walk in the park and see this thing near. I want see to—was mih first autumn—but I playing I ain't care before them bai start laugh at me and call me Newfie and Pole and Balgobin-come-to-town. Writerji ain't care about who laugh he, he want see this thing close, hold them leaves. So we laughing he, asking if he really want size up more geese because it gat geese in that park. We teking a drink on a picnic table in the park and Writerji disappear. Next thing he coming back with he hand full a them small sour apple. He can't believe all them apple falling on the grass and wasting. People wasteful in Canada he muttering over and over. Writerji want help to pick some nice green apple on them tree. Why? He thinking just like how yuh use green mango, or bilimbi, or barahar to make achaar and chatney why not green apple. And right then mango scarce in Toronto, cost a fortune. Them days was not like nowadays when you gat West Indian store every corner. Them days you only get fruits from the West Indies when anybody coming. But that apple-chatney taste good with them geese we bring for Prem and Kishore. Writerji didn't make no chatney though. He gat all dhem ideas but is me, Hermit and Prem and Kishore in they apartment making apple chatney! Not three cents dhat bai Writerji.

Anyway just after new year Hermit get a number for Writerji and same time a Vietnamese girl get pregnant and quit. So I talk to dhe boss and Writerji get tek on. Well is a factory making knockdown cardboard cartons up in Concorde by Steeles and Bathurst and is winter. We getting up five in the morning to reach for seven. Writerji get easy job. How he manage I ain't know. See I working on line. As fast as them boxes come off the line we gat to pack them on a crate. Yuh ain't even gat time to blow you nose or scratch yuh balls. If you tek a break while machine working cardboard pile up on you. Bai we only glad when machine break down every other day so we get an extra half hour or hour break. And them thing heavy. All Writerji gat to do is move them crates and strap them cardboard tight. Is not easy work but he could control things at he own pace. Dhe man whistling and singing while he working as though nuthing bother he. Lunch time he finding time to talk with them Vietnamese girls. Since I working in dhat factory them Vietnamese don't mix with nobody. At break time at nine they sit in a group one side in the factory, lunch time they sit there and afternoon break they sit there. Them two Vietnamese men watching Writerji carefully but soon he gat them girls laughing, and they saying hello now when they passing, and he know all they name.

Writerji dressing smart and comb he hair everytime he go to the toilet, soon he in the office talking to dhe payroll clerk, Annette, who uncle own dhe factory. She really pretty and she rarely come into the factory until Writerji start talking with she now and again during lunch time. The office mek with plexiglass and them office people could see everything happening in the factory. Soon she lending Writerji book. He just smiling when I ask he and saying is just literature. He trying to catch up on Canadian Literature.

Don't let mih tell yuh, dhem white man in the factory vex. They gat all them forklift and checker and loader and supervisor and manager jobs but Annette ain't bothering with dhem. Lunch time and break time them big-bais alone in the lunch room. Only Ravi with them. Ravi come from Sri Lanka and he is senior floor hand—them supervisor give he order and he give we order. And he feel superior. He working there long and feel he is white man too. He don't mix with we. All them floor hands Guyanese or Trini Indians, Sri Lankans or Vietnamese —and it look like everybody refugee. Soon the foreman start finding extra work for Writerji. As soon as Writerji finish strapping, he gat to come and help we on line, help with the forklift, clean up the factory floor, help with checking, help with dhis and dhat. Writerji still smiling but he hardly talking to Annette except when he gat to go and collect he paycheck from she every Friday afternoon. She and he talking on phone night time and weekend she coming for Writerji and they going for lunch or dinner. Writerji ain't going no place except work if he ain't get car. April coming and every morning at dhe bus stop Writerji grumbling about dhe blasted Canadian cold—and how dhe blasted foreman picking on he.

This lunchtime Writerji just done eating and he can't bear it. He walk straight in dhe office and give Annette a book, and spend two minutes chatting with she. And everybody could see what happening with dhem. Is love like first time. As soon as he come out dhe office and sit down next to me, the foreman come out the lunch room.

"Anand—this lunch room need cleaning and sweeping. Go and give it a clean out."

"I'm on lunchbreak now Tony." Writerji sounding sharp and everybody listening. The factory silent, nat a machine working. You know how in a factory everything close down because everybody get break same time.

"Well things slack now . . ."

Writerji cut him off and speaking louder, "Listen Tony, I said I'm on my lunch break. Talk to me after my break. Do you understand simple English?"

"You Paki teaching me about English?"

"I'm not a Paki. See you don't even know geography!"

"Alright smart ass. Clean and sweep this lunch room after break— here's the broom."

Writerji jump up and I get up too. I thinking he gun knock the foreman. "Let me tell you something Tony. You can take that broom and shove it. I don't eat in that lunchroom. Let the pigs who eat in there clean it up."

"You're fired man. You're fired." Writerji laugh loud and touch he waist.

"O course I'm fired! Jealous son-of-a-bitch! And you think I'm scared yeh! I had enough yeh. I quit anyway yeh!" He imitating the Canadian accent perfect perfect. I want laugh but, I thinking about meself so I hold in till Tony rush to the office. Writerji pick up he things and walk to dhe office, everybady watching as he bend down and whisper something in Annette ears and kiss she cheek. And she get up and follow he to dhe door. Night time Writerji tell me and Hermit he thinking about heading for New York. Same time Hermit lawyer just file my papers and he seh things look good fuh mih so I holding on. Writerji seh he ain't able with this cold and stupid Canadians, and he jus call he cousin in New York. New York warmer and things easier. The biggest joke is that he cousin give he two names in Toronto to contact in the "backtrack" ring to smuggle he across dhe border and one a dhe people is Hermit self!

Well next day late winter storm—one foot snow and cold cold. Minus fifteen degrees and with wind chill like minus thirty. Confusion on dhem road. People hardly go to wuk. I stay home. Writerji said he cut right card. He going to New York, he ain't staying for next Canadian winter. Two days later, is Friday, and everything running. Temperature warm up to minus two and road salted and clear, sunshine. Friday afternoon after work Annette come and she and Writerji gone out. Dhe man feel free like a bird. He stap grumbling about Canadian cold now he decide to head south. Half past five and place dark already. Me and Hermit done eat and looking news when, bam bam bam on dhe door. We think Writerji come back, forget he key or something. Is good thing is Hermit open dhe door. Two immigration officer get tip that an illegal alien name Anand living here. Man I nearly get heart attack. Hermit checking dhem ID and talking to them officer like is he own buddy and he invite them officer in for coffee—cold night for this work he telling them. Hermit say is just the two a-we live there. He show dhem ID and tell them how lawyer file paper fuh me. I not working he say just waiting for my case and he send me for mih passport and immigration papers. I sweating and praying dhat Writerji don't turn up then. After he tell dhem I ain't working I feeling better. I afraid I might say something wrang.

Finally them officer gone—apologize to we, man them men nice and pleasant and apologize. Hermit seh when dhem gane, don't let them smile fool yuh. Well is time to move Writerji. When Writerji come home is late. We looking TV and waiting fuh he but is he and Annette come in quiet quiet. Writerji laugh when he see we up. Well we gat to wait till next morning. We done know why dhem come in so quiet quiet like fowl thief. We mek excuse and hustle to bed closing we room door and left them on dhe settee.

Next morning Writerji blue when we give he dhe lowdown. He seh he certain is Tony. Yuh think Writerji would lie low after this! Dhat bai now get bad to go out. And Annette teking day off from work . . .

Yuh think is lil story we go through nuh. When Writerji ready fuh leave, is how you think he cross the border. Well a gun tell you but still secret. Yuh think Writerji can write dhis? Is in a container truck. Special container, forty-foot container. Them bai moving genuine shipment of furniture and personal effects to the States. Yuh know people always moving back and forth to States legally. A separate section in dhe front of dhe container conceal real good—double wall —to hold four people. That is how. Can't give more details as dhem bai still using dhe route. And Hermit seh less I know, less I talk. Well he didn't figure on Writerji. Writerji disappear underground in New York and is years we hear nothing about he. Next thing we know is novel out set in Guyana, and then dhem "Underground Stories" by a writer name S T Writerji! He mixing up place and incident between New York and Canada—who can tell what is what? But them thing real and only we know who is who. Writerji send Hermit book to mih house. When Hermit, Lena and them children come over Hermit quiet quiet. Is summer and we barbecuing in the backyard and dhem children running around, just like now. He find a corner and read that book right out. Nat a man disturb he. Lena surprise but nat me, dhat is dhe Hermit I know. When he done he shake he head and come over and tek a drink. Ask Lena and Katie. We drinking in mih house. Tears run down he eyes. No, that bai nat like Naipaul he seh. He mek we proud! Dhem days, dhem days right hey, mixup and sanaay, sanaay good like rice and daal, and nice hot seven curry with hot chatney. I read dhat book out, right out dhe night before and was same way I feel. Hermit tek a next drink—I gat a special bottle 12 year old Demerara Gold—and he come and sit next to me. Ask he when yuh see he. And he point to dhe front page. Writerji mek dedication—

To Hermit and Jones

—and he seh, "dhem days bai, dhem days is something else. See what we gain from dhem!" He close dhe book—just so and tears run down he face. Ask he, ask Hermit when yuh see him, ask him about dhat, about Writerji, about we.

Heads

At first I wasn't certain that he would meet me.

Hermit had cautioned, "The man has become somewhat of a recluse. Used to be very active five-six years ago, but suddenly dropped out of sight, popping up only momentarily in '92 when his last novel was published." But I was optimistic. I was a month in Toronto and settling in better than I expected, and Hermit was right. This time the circumstances were all different, I was seeing Toronto differently and liking it more. Perhaps, it must have had something to do with the fact that spring was in the air, officially a few days away, but already there were a few days of temperatures above zero—all the way to twelve. And poetry seemed to be sprouting out of everything around. It was a great way to begin this Toronto sojourn. I had returned this time for nine months and with a feeling that I would take a book away from this stay. I had figured on a novel and here was all this poetry! Perhaps there would be two books. The previous time I had spent six months and that stay gave me the stories of *Canada Geese and Apple Chatney*.

After I had introduced myself and indicated that I would like to meet him there was a long pause. I had that queasy feeling that he was about to decline, put down the phone when a baby started cooing. I didn't know that he had children, but then I knew nothing of his personal life except that he knew Devi. I had a suspicion that they might have shared something. Hermit had once seen him at an Indo-Caribbean function where he read poetry. He was with a woman whom Hermit believed to be his wife.

"I don't give interviews anymore," he said so softly that I had to strain to hear him, "and I don't have much time for literature right now."

"It is not for an interview—I would like to give you a copy of my most recent book, a collection of stories, *Canada Geese and Apple Chatney.*"

He could tell me to put it in the mail. The baby started cooing again.

"Ah, yes. I read a review of it in *Dayclean.*" That had not been a particularly good review; the reviewer felt that there was little or no depth to my characters, "characterless characters, a plotless plot and an impatience with atmosphere which seems more like the work of post-modernist(sic), slapdash writing!"

"Alright, how about tomorrow—say at 5 PM. Is that okay?" And he gave his address.

I had browsed through his *The Ghost of Bellow's Man* earlier in the day, reread the article on him in *Caribbean Daylight* and his piece, "Extending the Indian Tradition . . . " on himself. None of it quite prepared me. He was nothing like the photograph I had seen. I was expecting a person who was physically larger, a man with slicked down hair and someone very neat. When he opened the door and I saw the longish, unkempt hair I was startled, and he was in pajamas. Did he forget the appointment? Yet his lack of formality appealed to me, I felt as though I knew him immediately, as though we were twins. It was something I too would do.

We exchanged a few pleasantries and I gave him my book.

"Thanks," he took the book. "The cover is well done, can't promise you when I will read it but I am certainly looking forward to it. Judging from that review we may be doing something similar in our work . . " He continued looking at it silently, said, "Remember to sign it before you go—leave your address and phone number," he placed it on the desk in front of us. "So how did you get onto me?"

"I was intrigued by Odaipaul's article in *Daylight* and yours on your work, but perhaps more because of my cousin's wife, Devi, in New York. She's from the West Demerara. One day we were talking about writers and she mounted an extraordinary defence of your work. It was as though she knew you very well—though she didn't say so."

"Let's see, Devi Devi Devi—ah yes from my teaching days. There was a Devi from the West Bank in the Hindu society, I remember her now, a very decent and hard-working girl. Very active in the society— no I didn't think that I taught her though, don't think she was in one of my classes—so many students and such a long time ago!" He looked away and back at me, and without hesitating, "How's she doing?" I felt then for certain that there had been something between them. Her explanation of her acquaintance with him was almost exactly the same as his. I had suspected this since the time she called me and asked me who or what I thought was the "ghost" in his novel *The Ghost of Bellow's Man*—and especially when she had suggested that it could be this schoolgirl with whom he was in love. Not exactly a Lolita of South America! But why not her?

"She's fine. She's got two kids and lives in Queens not far from where I am." I had felt a twinge of jealousy before, as she was after all my cousin's wife, but meeting him now it didn't matter any more. I felt a greater kinship with him and with Devi than I felt with my cousin. And the past was the past. We all had our past, things we didn't want known, things best concealed for the peace-of-mind of all concerned.

I said: "I am intrigued by your usage of Indian aesthetics in your work and your comment that it is there in all our works, even in Selvon's and Naipaul's—consciously or unconsciously. Actually because of those articles and because of Devi I reread *Ghost*. I hadn't understood it till then. But I think, unlike you, I am working a bit more in the European tradition in my usage of plot and characterization, and language."

"Which is also very much another part of the Indian tradition. Attention to details of plot, more than plot—genealogies, which is what the *Mahabharata* is all about, and character, character development and/or stagnation permeate the other Indian epics, but because we are not familiar with our literary traditions we feel these things are from the European literary tradition. Where did the Europeans get it from? We are also talking about microtonal movements, small, or seemingly small but distinct shifts which call for careful reading, thinking-reading, which is lacking in the environment in which we live. We need to take the time off to consciously learn about ourselves. To hope that we will learn about ourselves through our writing or art is not enough. This places art above self and soul—sorry, no lectures. I haven't had enough of this lately . . . Let me get you a drink—tea, coffee . . . a cold drink?"

"Tea," I told him. He left the room. There were books on Indian philosophy, Indian literature and history on the shelves—Raja Rao, Narayan, Paramahansa, Tagore, Gandhi, the *Bhagavata Purana*— *Doctor Faustus, The Repeating Island,* Chopra, Eudora Welty, Truman Capote, Ismith Khan . . . I was fascinated. Would I let anybody, except someone who was close to me, into my study or even my home? Certainly not another writer whom I didn't know. A writer's books were private things, his secret tools. People learnt about your craft from what you read, what you had, did, how you lived. We all wrote about what we saw, heard or intuited but which one other person knew all of that, which one other person did we want to know all of that?

The baby started crying. There were murmurs and then he was talking to the baby as though allowing me time to study him in his room. Why? I had time to make out Thomas Mann on the cover of a book, upside-down on his desk, with a thin film of dust on it.

"Sugar and milk?" He peeped into the room.

"Yes." I was startled. I hadn't heard him approach.

"I took that chance—there are some phulourie here too, and some achaar." He was about to place the tray on the Mann book but stopped and held the book in one hand then put the tray down. "Last thing I was reading. Have you read it?" He turned the title to me, *The Transposed Heads.*

"No."

"An interesting story set in India involving a beautiful girl, a Brahmin boy and his lower-caste friend. The girl likes the strength of the lower-caste boy's body but the intelligence of the brahmin. They both want her. She marries the brahmin boy. Through a mix up in which the friends commit suicide, she implores the Divine Mother Kali to intercede and restore them and Kali agrees and gives the girl directions on how to do this, but the girl places the wrong heads on the bodies in bringing them back to life, and since her husband-head-on-the-body-of-the-lower-caste is able to argue successfully that the head is the essence and therefore he is really her husband, she finally gets the best of both, i.e. the head-intelligence of the brahmin and the firm body of the labourer, but only temporarily. The brahmin goes back to being a brahmin, and with little physical work, the body deteriorates while the frail brahmin-body-holding-the-lower-caste-head soon grows accustomed to hard work, and gets better . . . It's based on an Indian legend. The foremost and most popular of such stories of changing of heads is the story of Shiva giving Ganesha the elephant head. The whole concept of grafting, and transplanting, artificial insemination and so on was inspired by a western scientist having heard of the story of the Ganesha head . . . But I'm a slow reader, a slow writer too. I haven't read half the books I have—they are for show really, to create the aura of a writer's room; tone, atmosphere—the writer creating himself or characterizing himself, giving himself an artificial breath. Sometimes I think it is all just to convince myself that I am a writer! To convince myself that I didn't just stumble into writing and am stumbling through it, that I am a fraud."

There was a weariness in him. Had he lost hope?

"What about you? How did you come upon writing?" I was surprised by the alertness of the tone—the weariness gone in an instant.

"I always wanted to be a writer since I was in school. In school I used to read Shakespeare and Dickens and think, wouldn't it be great if I could create books like these, and other kids would have to study them, me, in classrooms! A conceit. but that's how I got hooked. My teacher always talked about how great a writer Shakespeare was. Shakespeare was a god to him. I wanted to be a god! And I went on and did English at UG—are you working on anything now?" I was not embarrassed about talking about what prompted the writing or the vanity of writing, but I was uncomfortable talking about me. I wanted to change the topic.

"Nothing at the moment, I'm learning parenting and I'm rejuvenating myself. I never know when I am going to write something, I can't plan my writing life and have a fixed schedule—say today I am going to write for three or fours hours, or for some length of time everyday for a year, or a month or even for a week. An idea, a story comes and then I must put aside all else and write. And it may be two, four, six years in between such bouts, though I may fool people, and sometimes myself, when asked what I am working on, and say vaguely that I am doing something, hiding in the writer's superstition about not wanting to discuss a work until it is finished—or I may hide in research! What about you? What are you working on? How do you write?"

"Presently I'm working with poetry, a collection. I would also be happy to leave Toronto after my stint here at the Consulate, with at least the idea of my next novel, if not the novel itself. As for the writing, I can only write with a fixed schedule—almost the exact opposite of you. And I read a lot. I think writers have to read a lot. Reading sustains me, gives me ideas, makes me aware of what others are doing."

He laughed, "Know the story about Sam Selvon and Naipaul? I will tell it to you as I heard it. Funny and seemingly simplistic. According to Jan Carew, in the old days when the West Indian Writers movement was picking up steam in London, Naipaul saw Selvon in the corridors of the BBC one day. Selvon had already published his classic *The Lonely Londoners* in an English dialect, Lamming had published his *In the Castle of my Skin,* and Naipaul just out with *The Mystic Masseur.* They used to meet once a week for a BBC Caribbean Programme and talk about their work, about anything but mostly about what they were reading and how they were using that. The programme was moderated by Andrew Salkey. Naipaul, of course, went to Oxford and it must have rankled that Selvon who didn't have a degree, didn't attend any university, was having his novel, in dialect, hailed as the West Indian classic on London. And Naipaul was probably wanting to show off his bookish erudition and to put down Sam. Sam was busy doing all sorts of odd jobs to make ends meet, and squeeze in writing time— how much time was there for reading? And, of course the West Indian writing community being small, they all knew of each other's situations.

So Naipaul comes up to Sam just before the start of one of their programmes and in his very proper English says, "Say old boy, What are you reading these days."

Sam responded like lightning, "Read? Read? Mih na read man? Nih nah readah, mih wan writah, nih a write!" So the story goes. Sam was always quick, witty and humorous and didn't pretend to be intellectually profound, didn't have to because he was very profound, and he couldn't hold a grudge against anyone. Naipaul seemed to have nursed his—in a review of Selvon's fifth book, *Turn Again Tiger* Naipaul wrote that Selvon did not have "the stamina for the full-length novel" and so had returned to the "undemanding form" of the short novel. Yet a few years ago before he died, when he was on the Neudstadt Prize Committee, Selvon nominated Naipaul for the prize. A pity you didn't know Sam, a great person—a great writer. Well Naipaul is a great writer too. I have always wondered why they never really published poetry . . .

"You know—I almost didn't agree to see you . . ." he trailed off again.

"Why don't you do interviews any more?"

"Well the things you say in an interview can come back to haunt you, or at the least make life uncomfortable for you—unless you are an Ishmael Reed! But you can say the things you want to say in an interview in fiction, even very contradictory things and not have to worry about anybody pinning you to it, you can shrug it off—it's fiction. And it is. Of course, if you are doing a Rushdie and dealing with Moslems or fanatics then you do have to worry not only about what you write but also your life! I agreed to meet you because I liked your brashness, and I felt myself in you even over the phone . . . Ever went to Miami?"

"No," I shook my head.

"Listen you've got to go, especially if you don't have the time to spare. They have a writers' programme in the summer. The space was good for me, it unleashed me from me and I sense that it will do the same for you. Ah that place, it gifted me a writer's dream of writing and memories and material! I'll give you the address and a contact . . ." Again he trailed off and smiled.

"I'll be here for the next nine months in Toronto. A stint at the consulate—a sort of National Service so I can officially graduate from UG. But when I return to New York make sure you visit me." I wanted to make a gesture and I could only think of her—"Let me know in advance so I can invite my cousin and Devi—they are over regularly." I don't know why I said that but the moment it came out, I knew it was the right thing to do.

"Yes. It would be good to see her and her family." We exchanged addresses.

At the door he said, "If for any reason I don't get to visit you in New York or we don't meet in a hurry, come and see me when you become famous—which may be sooner than you think. We can do an interview then." There was no irony. I believed. Somewhere behind him there was a subdued coaxing, that talky-talk adults use when communicating to newborns, and then there was fulsome, uninhibited baby laughter.

Arriving

You know, by some intuitive sense, when you have arrived at some extraordinary time in your life. You know when the things you have been expecting and hoping for are happening faster than you anticipate—when those things seem to spring literally out of the blue. And you know that only when those times and things are almost on you. Sitting in the lounge of Toronto's Pearson Airport and waiting to board the Air Canada flight to Miami, it suddenly dawned on me that this was one of those times.

*

There was that other time years ago. I was riding my motorcycle: this on the streets of a Georgetown suburb on the South American coast, approaching from the east side of an intersection on which I had the right of way. A car approaching from the south and going north had paused, as though about to stop. I was in the middle of the intersection when something made me look around. The car, which I had seen slowing down, was inches and seconds from crashing into me. I thought: this is it—you're dead. I gave up, letting go of the handlebars. That letting go saved me. Had I held on I would have ended up under the car with the motorcycle.

There is no recollection to this day of the impact, or of somersaulting twenty-five feet in the air, or of landing half inside the nearby ditch. There I was on my stomach looking at the crowd gathering around the car and peeping at the motorcycle compressed under it, and wondering why nobody was coming to my assistance. You notice all the minor details in such situations, like it being a warm day, like the ditch having no water because it was nearing the end of the long dry season. Another car, which had been about half a mile behind me just before the accident, pulled up and the driver came straight towards the ditch. That was when the crowd must have realized I was not under the car, mashed like the motorcycle. The driver did not hesitate but had me placed in her car—a brand-new Mazda—though I was bleeding and couldn't move my left leg.

"I thought you dead," she said as she drove to the hospital. I was beginning to feel the pain and was thinking, looking at the blood in her car, how how can I repay you—or thank you? This is an extraordinary kindness—you're so beautiful! I was certain that I had seen her before; her shoulder-length black hair waving in the wind that came in through her open window, half of one long black eyelash visible, one amber-brown eye when she turned intermittently, and the edges of her mouth, and the thin, beautiful slightly down-curved nose.

"One moment you were in the distance in front of me—the nickel fenders of your motobike sparkling in the sunshine, the road deserted except for the two of us, and the next this car from nowhere—and you somersaulting in the air, oh maybe twenty-five, thirty feet: your white shirt billowing out, your trousers in the winddrag like a cloud swirling in the blue sky, and then all these people appearing out of nowhere around the car and peeping and peeping and peeping . . . it happened quickly and I was wondering why nobody saw you in the air and where you landed. I never liked that intersection, and all those men in the beergarden guzzling beers all hours of the day . . . and you weren't wearing a helmet! You're lucky . . . " I did possess a helmet, but because the helmet law was not being enforced I rode without it.

At the hospital, when the orderlies put me on the stretcher she accompanied them and me until I was looked at, and she made the phone calls for me, stayed at my side until my father came. I have never thanked her properly, but I am sure my father did as they spent awhile outside talking while my thigh was being stitched up. My father spoke glowingly of her afterwards. It was a month before I could walk again without any great discomfort, and before I could return to work.

It was not until that time that I came to learn how much my father loved me. I had always thought he never really cared about me: it was not that he hated me or disliked me—it was just that I was a child, definitely not a favourite child, and he was my father and that was it. That first week at home while I recuperated, my father did not go to work. He cooked soups and broths and made various foods to get my strength back up as I had lost a lot of blood. He was a great cook and everyone of our relatives knew that. Going to the bathroom or toilet did not need much assistance as there were the walls I could hold on to, but in that first week, it was comforting to know that he was just a call away if I needed him. Many parts of me died that month I was at home, but many other parts of me were also born. It was one of the fullest times of my life.

In the mornings, by the time I had finished with my bath, all the others would have left and the house would be empty. I would lie propped up in bed near the window looking out east and read. More often I listened to the unimaginable, indescribable mornings and early afternoons: wind prattling, whispering, singing, roaring in the coconut branches nearby and in the leaves of trees; starapple, almond, jamoon and that golden apple closest to my window rippling like water over rocks in a stream: the birds; kiskadees exulting "kis kis ka dee," and at other times their tentative "eevah eevah eevah," half notes, half calls, half responses—those kiskadees had the widest range of notes and songs—and there were the tanagers; "blue sakies," "cashew sakies" and "coconut sakies" as we called them, and wrens, grackles and "jumbie birds." I was starting to learn which birds sang at what times of the day, and under what conditions. And there was always the sky with its illusive shades of blue, and the coconut-jelly-coloured clouds. Butterflies visited the flowers and frolicked around in the grass. It was August-September, and the rains were yet to make an appearance.

On the day, that first week, when the man whose car had hit me came, I was seething, angry because he was wrong, had run a stop sign and I was in pain because of this. He apologized but offered an explanation: he thought because I had looked at him before I entered the intersection that I was yielding—and he was not familiar with the area, and hadn't seen the stop sign—but he would make some kind of restitution if we did not press charges: he could lose his licence and his livelihood, maybe the car itself, since it would be held for months until the case came up in court, by which time the police would have cannibalized the car, "selling" parts to their friends. It was known to happen. The safest place for a car or any item in a dispute was as far away from "police safekeeping" as possible. He was a poor man from the country, using his car as a taxi on a rare trip into the city. His brakes were defective and his insurance coverage minimal, so he had taken the sideroads to bypass the traffic police on the major roads to get out of the city. It was well known that once they stopped a car they would find any reason to extract a bribe.

My father listened. There would be no charges he said, but perhaps the man would like to restore the motorcycle. The man agreed. But looking at him and his old, battered Morris car we knew he couldn't afford to do so, and my father was giving him a way out. The man promised to come the next week.

I was seething when the man left, my father barely bothering to take his name and address. My father said quietly, "More important you well—no money could pay for dhat, no money in this world—nothing son. Leh he go. Yuh foot will heal, you'll be ok. Your're lucky." I knew my father was right but part of me still wanted the man to pay.

"Could'a been me in his position," he said reflectively, "and dhe lady? She didn't think of blood in she cyaar—yuh health first! And her cyaar seat, dhe carpet? She wouldn't take anything, wouldn't hear of it. And you think I could repay her for dhat? No son, no . . . let him go." I knew vaguely that there was more to letting the man go: a subversion of the racism nobody would talk about publicly. The man was Indian. Almost all of the traffic cops were men of African ancestry—almost all of the taxi drivers they stopped and harassed were of Indian ancestry.

Through everything, in that first week my respect for my father deepened. I saw only part of the picture. My father saw something fuller, more whole. And that thing about this Other Thing being more important than money, which he had been teaching and practising all his life, suddenly became as clear as the blue sky outside, as graspable as the birdsongs, as palpable as the silences touching my thinking when he was taking a nap and there was no wind, and the branches were still, and there was no birdsong or barking dog, no cockcrow echoing from afar, no screech of rubber on asphalt in the distance, nor any whisper from the ocean beyond. In the afternoons various friends and relatives came, the boys from the office, the girls standing around talking, sitting on the edge of my bed, browsing through the books on my bookshelf, a chance to satisfy their curiosity about my reclusiveness, their laughter ringing through the house. But while I looked forward to these evening visits, I also looked forward to those silences and those spaces which my father gifted me, and in a way guarded for me. My father had long known that I was a poet—the music and poetry coming from him—and that I had written a novel. He had given me the space for that too.

Perhaps he knew when I asked for my notepad and my pen that my story was being born, and my life as a storyteller—but I could never hope to match my father as a storyteller. Where had I learnt that my father was my idol and to compete with your idol was to unmake your idol, and in the process unmake yourself? An old Sanskrit saying, "Pita deo bhawa, mata deo bhawa"—your father your god on earth, your mother your god on earth? Later I was to come on Vidia Naipaul and his offering in his introduction (after his father died) to his father's stories.

I wrote two stories in this time, both ostensibly about death; the first leading into the next, into the one I really wanted to record: a story in which a son from a rural area, more privileged than his other siblings, and a favourite of his father, rejects all that his father and his community stood for, but in the end realizes that his rebellion was harming him and those around him most. When he decides to return home to the country and the land, from the city and his dissipation there, it is just at the time his father is breathing his last. That story was published and republished in both Guyana and Trinidad. In it I was trying to say all that I wanted to say to my father but couldn't bring myself to articulate: that I was returning to that continuity of consciousness and thought he had offered but which I had rejected in my obsession with the cynicism of the voices of my other education, the voices of the west.

It was a leap forward for me into ancestral and preancestral consciousness and forms. Later, much later, I saw that that story was really about the interstices of time through which my father was allowing me a quantum leap. It was one of those times when you know that you know, that you had arrived at an extraordinary period in your life and had not been aware until now.

*

I had arrived early at the Pearson airport because Hermit and Lena who were giving me a ride to the airport were taking the girls to spend a week with Lena's parents in the country. In the four months I had been staying with them, Lena had grown on me; as Hermit had said in his letter, she was an extraordinary woman. I had had this notion that for a Hindu of our generation, though having been born and living all our lives in the west but with a certain passion for Indian philosophy and culture, the difference with a white North American woman would prove too great for any stable long-term relationship—let alone a lifelong commitment in marriage. Lena and Hermit had put a big dent in that notion. They had opened up not only a new world and a new set of possibilities for me, but had also freed a part of me which I had closed and had guarded doggedly since Annette . . . which was a long time ago. Annette belonged to that first, short unpleasant visit to Toronto which I believed I had finally put behind me.

But one night when we were alone at Jones's place he had asked, "So wha happen with dhe thing in dhe factory? Yuh remember? Dhat girl really like yuh head!"

"Old story."

"Old wine cure better! Everybady think yuh would'a married dhe damn girl—and she could'a sponsor yuh. Could'a save yuh years of hardship! Where was yuh brains, in yuh dick?" Jones laughed. Hermit barely smiled.

"Remember I was illegal here and in New York—I didn't tell her I was leaving Toronto until I was in New York—it probably wasn't hard for her to guess my situation anyway—but she thought I had another girl in New York . . . O well some things don't work out."

The girls and Hermit waved as I went through customs. Then, as though just remembering, Lena raised a hand. It wasn't a wave, it looked like a hand held up in a benediction, the blessing of a guru. In that moment I felt I had entered a different time—a time you know has come again . . .

The lounge was empty when I entered but soon there was more than a trickle of people arriving. It was clear this would be a full flight. I was surveying the passengers as they came in, wondering who would be sitting next to me when a woman in a white pantsuit came in. I thought: not bad looking for her age, an ex-dancer. The pants did not go all the way to her ankles but ended between ankles and calves, emphasizing the calf muscles, and she seemed to walk on her toes. As she was about to sit there was a boarding call and then an announcement for a Kelly-something to report to the check-in desk outside. She looked up and hurried out: too bad, probably a standby and the flight is full!

The plane was full but the seat next to me was still unoccupied. I was looking outside at the loaders when I heard the overhead rack above my head being closed. When I turned it was her, the woman in the white pantsuit. She smiled and I nodded and smiled too as she sat beside me. Soon we were taxiing to the runway and I turned to the window to look at the objects being passed, fascinated, as always, as we left the ground and the familiar landmarks behind. She too was looking past me out the little window and I pulled in so she could get a better view. The lake was a deep green and then an aqua-green—a cooling green, the white sails of boats were bloated with the wind and there was a thin line of white streaking the water—the wake of a powerful motorboat.

"Beautiful, isn't it?" I said still looking out.

"Yes—Toronto is a beautiful city. Ontario a very pretty place." There was silence except for the drone of the engine. We were still climbing, heading into clouds.

"I thought you would not make the flight, I saw you leaving after the announcement," I turned to her.

"Yes. What a morning! First we had a puncture on the Highway. I had to get a taxi from there. Then I forgot to put my name and a tag on one of my suitcases. Customs pulled it off the check-in line . . ."

"Lovely—your accent—not from Toronto or from the States?"

"No," she said, "how can you tell?"

"The lilt in your voice is something I have heard but can't quite place, I know it is definitely not North American—closer to but not British." I laughed, "And you didn't say Torono for Toronto."

"South Africa," she said.

"Far! Holiday? Or do you live here now?"

"A rare holiday to these parts, in fact my only trip to North America but it is good to be returning home. Do you live here, or was this too a holiday?"

"I live in New York but I was born in South America—Guyana. I will be in Toronto until the end of this year."

"I sensed that you were not born here—you're too friendly to be North American."

"Really?"

"Yes. In my experience North Americans are too cold, reserved, perhaps too obsessed with themselves. O dear me—I forgot to introduce myself, I am Kelly," she gave me her hand. There were freckles on it and short blond hairs. Her fingers were not tapered nor were they stubby, and the fingernails were short. Her hand was warm and firm. There was a twinkle in her blue-grey eyes. At this proximity the facial lines were visible. Because of her trim figure and the distance in the lounge she had appeared to be in her late thirties or early forties, but perhaps she was closer to fifty. There were freckles on her face and the skin had that leathery look you find in people who have lived all their lives in the tropics. It was a skin texture I had not seen in the last several years in New York or Toronto, but I knew it well from far away and long ago.

"Yes. I remembered it from the announcement though I missed the last name."

"Waithe."

"Not w-e-i-g-h-t?"

"No. W-a-i-t-h-e."

"I know, I am teasing you—I live in North America now and I could be excused for spelling it even as w-a-i-t." We laughed.

"And I am Anand Sharma."

"Write if for me —spell it," she smiled.

There was a card in my wallet, "Here—you can keep this."

"Ah yes. Anand, a beautiful name."

"You got it as though you knew it all your life. You pronounced it like an Indian! Here I get Aaynan almost all the time!"

"There are Indians in South Africa—And yes there are Indians in the Americas too—Columbus!" Laughter again. "It was so funny in my first week. Still is, even now. I heard wader for water . . . "

"Pennies for cents," I added.

"Yes, yes and Tomaayto for Tomato . . . "

"You too! In New York it's worse. There's gad for god, bax for box . . . "

"And football for a game where men run with the ball in their hands, or butt each other like rams most of the time, look through each other's legs for it . . . what we call football they call soccer." In her laughter she tapped my wrist lightly.

"It was the same for me when I came first—funny indeed."

"We do have something in common!" She added. I was about to say something similar.

"The voices of our British education," I said and she nodded. We had become friends and had slipped into a familiarity and comfort in which friends can say nothing to hurt each other; we didn't want to do anything to change that. Her fingers, after she had tapped my wrist remained on the armrest, barely touching my forearm. We were both conscious of this and the energy and calm flowing through. We couldn't look at each other then, or speak. A long stillness followed. There were thick white clouds outside. I was seeing and not seeing. The cabin became darker. Then there was a, "pung" and the fasten-your-seat-belt sign lit up. If our bodies could remain that way! I had not unbuckled my seat belt since takeoff but she had.

"This is your captain: we are experiencing a bit of turbulence. . . The magic was starting to ebb even before she removed her hand to fasten her seat belt. She placed her elbow on the armrest, hand in lap, the edge of a sleeve touching the edge of my sleeve. That communicative silence came again as the plane bounced through darker clouds this time. The cabin was getting noticeably cooler. There was rain, lightning.

"I don't like flying—one of the reasons I hardly ever leave South Africa. My cousin had to coax and coax to get me to take this trip. I didn't really want to."

"Then why did you?"

"My husband died nine months ago. We had been married for close to thirty years and everyone thought a break would be good for me. I knew him since we were in high school. I've never known another man. But his death was not sudden, he was sickly so I had time to sort of get used to the idea and I had my work." There was no self-pity but she was making an effort to conceal a regret.

"I'm sorry. That's a long time . . ."

"Well," she waved her hand, "so I decided I would humour my

cousins and all my friends who felt I needed a break—but life goes on. Toronto is nice and I had a wonderful stay—but it feels good to be going home." A smile had returned to her face, our connection clicking back into place.

"Must have been quite a change, the end of apartheid."

"Yes and for the better. It was inevitable . . ."

"Have you thought of moving to Canada—with your husband gone . . ."

"No. I don't want to. South Africa is home for me, will always be home for me, the only place I want to live. And after apartheid, I feel as free as I haven't felt in decades. Now it is easier not to have to walk around feeling guilty. And I cannot be responsible for what other white people did, I can only be responsible for my own actions."

I remembered, "This is an amazing coincidence. Only recently I read a brilliant essay by a white South African woman—a Brenda Cooper—on South African literature. And she mentions something about that—why should she feel any guilt for what she didn't do . . . I think she is at the University of Cape Town. Have you heard of her? What part of South Africa are you from? Cape Town?"

"Yes, I'm from Cape Town too, but I've never heard of her." The fasten-seat-belt-light turned off with another "pung."

"Then you probably wouldn't have heard of Reshard Gool—a South African writer of Indian ancestry. He wrote a novel called, *Cape Town Coolie*. What is the most outstanding thing about Cape Town?"

"For me, Table Mountain. If you love hiking, or just the scenery, you would love it. Many tourists go there. It is above the city and you can see out to the cape—really beautiful . . . you would love it—I see on your card that you are a writer—do you write poetry?"

"Yes."

"I would be glad to read some of your work."

I told her I hadn't published a collection yet, though I had a manuscript in my suitcase. Perhaps when she was next in North America . . .

"Yes—that would be good but it is most unlikely that I would come this way again. It is expensive for one and a very long flight. But if ever *you* come to South Africa why don't you come and visit me . . ." She reached for her bag and searched for a card. "Here—I recently changed my phone." She wrote the new number at the back of the card and gave it to me. Kelly Waithe's Pet Training School. An idea was forming in my head.

"We arrive in Miami at one—your flight leaves at a quarter to seven. That's almost a five-hour wait. Why don't you come out and see something of Miami you will have at least four hours with enough time to get your flight to Cape Town—and you can see something in that time . . ."

"But I don't know Miami. I have no one there and I hear it is a dangerous city."

"This is my first trip to Miami but I have several maps and a very good idea of the area around the university campus where I will be staying. All I have to do is register when I get there, get my suitcases out of the way and we could explore the campus—I understand from an acquaintance who was there that it is a very pretty campus. And it's only fifteen minutes from the airport—I have all the information in my bag—the university sent a complete package. And it is safe on the campus . . ."

She was assessing the idea, and me: What did I want? Would I try to seduce her? Did I want to seduce her? "You have nothing to fear. And it will cost you nothing to be able to see something of the place. I will have to take a taxi anyway, and as you point out you may never come this way again."

She laughed, "Sounds good. We'll see by the time we land." I could feel her debating, should she or shouldn't she?

"So how long are you going to be at the University of Miami?"

"A month, almost five weeks. They have a writers' summer pro-gramme where various writers meet, a space to write, away from the hurly-burly of the day-to-day grind, a place to have our works cri-tiqued by our peers and by scholars present, read from our works—ex-pound on the things which inform our writing, learn what others are doing . . . I haven't been involved in anything like it before but I understand that it is a great stimulus for the muse . . ." Lunch was being served. There was a clinking of utensils and a tired look on the face of the flight attendant by the time she got to us, straining to push the stained aluminium cart before her. The wheels were not moving easily and the cart was a tight fit in the aisle. The lunch she served contained a chicken sandwich. I was about to ask for something else but when I looked up and saw the effort behind the thin smile I changed my mind. It was no sense making her day more pressured when there would be no real alternative—and there was salad and some fruits on the tray, and there would be coffee or tea. That was enough. Kelly took the sandwich when I gave it to her and shared her carrot cake.

"Are you vegetarian?" We were sipping coffee and the pilot announced that in half an hour we would be landing. Our approach to Miami airport would be from the east, over the Atlantic. We were already descending through a layer of clouds.

"Yes," I replied, "Non-smoker too, but I occasionally take a drink or two—on very special occasions; wedding toasts etc." I realized that perhaps I was courting her. She was not an unattractive woman and yet not the woman I would normally be attracted to, but there was a special bond between us. It could have been the proximity, or the sense of excitement a journey to a new place brings, or perhaps it was that clarity of thought which allows us to see past externals, to connect to the humanity in others, which an entry into these windows of timelessness affords. Perhaps it was also a response to my perception of her own physical fitness.

"Somehow when I first saw you in the airport in Toronto, I thought you were an athlete, a ballet dancer to be more exact."

"You've got good eyes and intuition. I was a ballet dancer in my earlier years and for many years I taught dance. I still teach a class on occasion."

"How did the pet training come about?"

"I have, on and off, always had a dog and friends and acquaintances would always comment how well behaved my dogs were. How was I doing it? That started it and I had done my degree in psychology, it was easy to go to animal psychology . . ."

"This is intriguing. So what happens to your classes while you are here—and your dog?"

"My daughter will look after the dog. She's a wonderful dog and I miss her. My daughter lives with me. She's at university. The pet training classes are shut down while I am away. This trip I had to plan months in advance—to be able to close the classes for this long—five weeks. A week before and a week after I return, to give me time to settle back in."

"There's been a dog story in my head for years, which I have never quite been able to write. I just seemed to be missing a connection. Maybe this! An extraordinary coincidence! What in your experience is the most common misconception about dogs? What is the most important thing to know about them?"

"Well most people want their dogs to be more than a pet, to be a companion. People, and the majority of dog owners who come to me are mainly women, want the dog to take the place of their spouses and lavish 'love,' affection, on their dogs, plain spoiling them. A dog is basically a pack animal. Dog owners forget that we have taken the dog out of its natural habitat where it would run with others of its kind, where there is always a leader who decides what the pack does, how each animal functions in the group. The house dog sees the 'owner' and the other humans around as its substitute pack, and it is looking for leadership—firm, decisive leadership—at all times. And if there is not that decisive leadership, then it tries to assume that leadership, become head of the pack. Even when there is strong leadership some dogs try every so often to challenge that leadership."

I was fascinated by her knowledge. This which seemed so logical and easy to understand I would never have figured out if she had not put it so succinctly. What could I hold forth on, as passionately? What could I give in return? Was anything more necessary on this path we were journeying down, and from which we could not turn back?

"Would you like to sit at the window?"

"No no," she said, "I can see from here." She was leaning a little towards me. We were on the right side of the plane and the land was visible to us. The plantations of South Central Florida and then the Everglades. Grass, clumps of trees, the hammocks and then we were circling to the east then turning west towards the airport, over the clear blue ocean which turned into a pale lemon green closer to the long strip of sand. The bathers seemed touchable, and the highway and roofs coming up, the land, the tarmac; a sudden bump, then another and the rubber and asphalt screamed.

"Miami," I said.

"Yes Miami," she repeated. "Anand, thank you for giving me a chance to see a bit of Miami."

"No. Thank you for a most remarkable flight. South Africa Air will be looking after your baggage?" I asked, and she nodded. "We'll reconfirm your flight and check-in time, then we'll collect my baggage." She nodded again. The plane was turning towards the terminal. The first thing which struck me as we came out was the heat. As we wheeled the suitcases through the doors, a taxi came up almost immediately.

"University of Miami," I said when the driver placed the suitcases in the trunk. He looked puzzled. "The University of Miami in Coral Gables," I said slowly this time. I had read that many of the Miami taxi drivers were recent immigrants. Perhaps he was from Haiti or Africa and was not too familiar with the language. "I have the directions," I added. The university had provided a good map of the route from the airport to the check-in suite and I had memorized it. "South on LeJuene to Ponce De Leon Boulevard. Right into Ponce De Leon to the University, right into Merrick Drive." When we got in I gave him the map I had. He looked at it nodded and gave it back to me. "It's fifteen minutes," I added. He nodded again. When I saw him following the large overhead sign out of the airport to LeJuene I relaxed, but I was still tense and alert. Alone I would not have worried but I was conscious that I was responsible for another person, in a city in which I was also a stranger—even though I had for weeks been studying a street map and memorising the directions of the major roadways. There was hardly any traffic on the road and the houses and area we passed were well maintained. The sun was bright. The huge overhead sign at the end of LeJuene gave directions to US 1—South Dixie Highway—and Ponce De Leon Boulevard. "Right into Ponce," I said. He nodded. Suddenly we were passing streets and there were no street names. "Are there no street names?"

"On the ground—Coral Gables' a unique place in Miami," he half turned and smiled. The names of streets were etched on white slabs of concrete on the pavements. I glanced at Kelly. She too smiled.

"First place I am seeing this." Again the driver half turned and smiled. The trip took twelve minutes. As soon as we turned into Merrick Drive we saw the cardboard sign—Writers Institute Registration. The asphalt parking lot was hot. Kelly, still silent, helped with my carry-on bag to the door of the hospitality suite. When we entered it was cool, almost cold inside.

"Good afternoon." I said.

A sandy-haired woman turned her head quickly, "Hello," looking up over the top of her gold-rimmed glasses, then got up and extended her hand. It was cold, soft and limp. "I'm Judith Bondar."

"Yes, I saw your name on one of the brochures. Anand Sharma,"

"I guessed." She ticked my name on a list and looked at the boy of about ten whom I hadn't seen in the far corner of the room, "The one with the 'strange name'." A girl of about five was sleeping on the sofa next to him. "My son Andy had difficulty pronouncing your name," she said as the boy gave me a kit with my name on it. A dark-haired, woman wearing glasses came through the door with a suitcase. "Hi— please make yourself at home, I'll be with you in a short while," Judith Bondar told her, smiling at the newcomer, then turned back to me, "the kit has various bits of information about the campus, a map, library rules, a pass to the cafeteria, etc., a schedule of the programme. I'll be here until seven tonight if you have any questions—my home and office number are also listed. Tomorrow at one there's an orientation session in the International Scholars Service Building. Ah—

you're one of the lucky ones, the odd person, so you have a flat all to yourself—there are two bedrooms so you can use whichever you want, or both. Your are in 23 N on the ground floor—just across," she pointed. "These are your keys. The larger one is for the outer door, the smaller one for your room door. There's a refundable key deposit— $15.00. If you don't have change now you can pay it at the English Department office tomorrow . . ." The words tumbled out of her as though she was in a great hurry. I gave her the deposit. "Like I said, I'm here until seven—somebody will be here after seven for those coming on later flights. Call if there are any questions." I nodded, "Thanks," and turned. Kelly was standing near the door with my suitcases.

When we were outside the door, I told her, "Let me just get rid of these suitcases and get the campus map."

The drapes were open, light streamed into the apartment. There was something uplifting about the light. I dragged my suitcase into the first bedroom. When I turned around, Kelly was behind me with my bag. She put it down near my suitcase and sat on the bed.

"It's a neat little apartment—warm isn't it?" She said. I turned the airconditioner on and sat on the bed next to her, opened the kit and located the list of taxis services and restaurants in the vicinity, and studied the map of the campus.

"I feel famished," I said, "what about you?"

"Yes." Were we courting each other? I glanced at her, then stood up. She was a friend and a companion I had never known before, and yet had always known. This was more important for me. "Let's go and get something to eat on campus and walk around. Would you like to freshen up first?"

"No. I'm fine." And while I was closing the apartment door she looked at the sky; birds we couldn't see in the tree nearby were singing, "You know they say you should never leave a strange airport in a strange land with a stranger!"

I laughed as we started walking across the campus towards the little lake. "Are we strangers?"

"No," she said, taking my arm. We walked wordlessly, in one of those moments of silence in which everything sings; the light wind in the trees, even the cars in the distance: it was a silence when every movement became a dance—the flicker of leaves and twigs, the flight of a bird, the swaying of fig roots in the air, the waving of palm branches. I had come home. It was years since I had seen so many coconut palms, real palms in the earth and not in pots in public places encased in glass and concrete. And the saman trees were in bloom, red and yellow samans, huge cassia trees with their blossoms hanging down like golden tresses. In more than a decade I had not seen anything as beautiful. Almost fifteen years!

At one point we were crossing a bridge over a canal draining the little lake on the campus ground, when a sudden noise from the black water startled us; we stopped and stared at the ripples on the water. There was another sudden noise and a shoal of large fish leaped into the sunshine and then back into the lake again.

"Wow!" was all she said for both of us.

The restaurant was closed but one of cafeterias was open. We ate on the northern shore of the lake under a row of trees. There were ducks in the lake and herons, a green-backed and two big blue herons fishing near the shore among the water lilies; a light breeze took the discomfort out of the warm afternoon, the fountain in the lake sounded like a distant drizzle. From the pool near Whitten International Centre a woman was climbing to the topmost dive board. It was a long way up. She stood on the tip of the board, perhaps thirty or forty feet up, and waited, concentrating. There were huge pine trees outside the pool compound behind her, the green needles as backdrop emphasising the almost naked, cream-bronzed body. She left the board in a smooth plunge. The concrete wall around the pool blocked our vision of her entry into the water. Fish leaped in the distance from the lake and a bird twittered over our heads. I look up startled. We were sitting under rows of sapodilla trees bearing tiny green sapodillas.

"Do you have this tree in Cape Town? It's the sapodilla, also known as the naseberry. A fruit native to Central and South America. It's the sweetest, most delicious fruit I've eaten."

"It looks a bit familiar—we probably know it by a different name."
She looked intently at the tree.

"What was the funniest incident you have had with the pets in your
school?"

"Oh it was with a dog. During a break one day I was stooping on
the grass, petting a poodle. A large alsatian was running round and
round and must have scared the poodle. The alsatian was a new dog
in the school. Suddenly I felt a warm liquid running down my back.
The alsatian was peeing on me! The owner was speechless. Finally
she came over and apologized profusely to me. I told her not to
worry—the dog was only staking his claim so to speak, marking out
his territory. Most animals do that in one way or another, mark their
territory by leaving their scent someplace. The woman never came
back! I have always wondered if the problem was with the dog or the
dog-owner!" She laughed and then looked up intently at the tree
again, then at her watch; she got up, looking around presumably for
the garbage bin, which was to our left. I dropped our refuse in. "We
can walk around the lake—on our way back?" she asked.

"Yes," I answered and took her outstretched hand. We walked
slowly.

"It is very beautiful here. In some ways it feels like home," she
said, pausing in the grass near a cluster of laden coconut trees. The
nuts were of a yellowish hue and just over our heads. "Years since I
have strolled on a campus," she continued almost in a whisper. We
walked under a few tall tamarinds, the ripe tamarind pods, rust brown
where they had fallen on the grass. I could write books here I felt;
fiction, even criticism and poetry. It was half past three when we returned to the apartment.

"Should I call a taxi now?"

"Not just yet, let me freshen up."

"I have fresh towels in my suitcase, let me get you one." I went into
the bedroom and unzipped a suitcase. Two books tumbled out. I gave
her a towel and when she went to the bathroom I took one of the books

out to the sitting-room table and sat on the sofa thinking of something to write. It seemed I waited a long time. Nothing appropriate came.

"I had a shower," she said looking at her watch, "it's a long trip to South Africa." She sat on the sofa, nodded towards the phone; I called a taxi.

"This is for you." I gave her a copy of *Canada Geese and Apple Chatney.* "My most recent book, a collection of short stories. Unfortunately I don't have extra copies of my novel."

"Thank you," she flipped the pages. "Well aren't you going to autograph it?"

"That is only for celebrity writers."

"Then for the time you become a celebrity writer!" The car horn mingled with our laughter in the apartment. "That was quick."

I picked up her bag and the book, "I'll come with you to the airport—wouldn't want anything happening to you."

"You don't have to you know—but thank you," and laughingly as an after thought as we exited the apartment, "would you be able stop what could happen from happening by your presence?"

"No. But if something were to happen while I were safe . . . the airport," I said to the driver as we got in, "South African Air." We travelled in silence. I was thinking of something I could write in the book. She paid the taxi driver before we got out. After she had checked in we sat in the public waiting area looking out over the tarmac. She placed an arm through mine, leaning her head on my cheek. Her hair was still moist from the shower. There was a faint scent of soap, a scent I hadn't smelt since I left Guyana. I was still thinking of a line to write for her, conscious that people were arriving from various flights, heading down to the baggage claim area and soon out into the city. This airport was a place for transit. Not really a place of arrival, but eternally a place of departure. Even those who had just arrived had left something behind, and then soon left this point of arrival behind too. I wrote.

Kelly

For this journey to this point of departure

From that to this self's arrival—
This sunshine of souls
With thanks and love.
Anand—Miami.

It was time. Before going through the security gate she stopped, placed an arm around my back, and kissed me. "Thank you for the best day of my holiday, the best day in many many years. Whenever, if ever you come to South Africa, I will put aside all else for you. Know you will always have a friend there." I put my arm around her and kissed her. And she kissed me again.

"Goodbye," I said and gave her the book.

"Goodbye." She turned from beyond the security gate and her hand went up. It wasn't a wave. It was something I knew. The blessing of a guru. For the first time in my life I couldn't form an opinion or even an impression of a woman, of another person. Was an opinion necessary?

We strive to still our minds and thoughts in yoga. Sometimes we succeed. Sometimes we don't. Sometimes our minds and thoughts still themselves. Sometimes something Other stills them. Who could say what was happening . . . ?

All I knew was that we would meet again in another time, another place; on another body, another head, another face.

Glossary

Aarti	The concluding ceremony in a Hindu prayer service.
Aja	Paternal grandfather.
Ajee	Paternal grandmother.
Angrezi babu	An English Indian or Indian British; often derogatory.
Ashram	Spiritual retreat.
Baap re baap	An exclamation.
Bhai	Or bai, brother.
Bhajan	Hymn.
Bhaarat	India.
Bhariat	Or bharaat, a wedding procession.
Bhunoya	Sister's husband.
Bigan	Eggplant.
Bollywood	A term used to denote the Indian film capital, Mumbai, formerly Bombay.
Brahmini	Female of the learned and priestly caste.
Chacha	Paternal uncle.
Chupchaal	Card game whist. Literally silent leading.
Churkis	Small tuft of hair left on the shaven heads of members of some Indian religious orders.
Dhaal	Daal.
Dhaar	Water or liquid, often offered from the palms of the hands, in worship.
Dharm Patni	Wife, according to the ethics of Dharma.
Dholak	A hand drum.
Dhoons	Hymns.
Ganesha	"Elephant-headed" god of wisdom.
Havan khund	A container, or metal vessel in which the ritual fire for an Indian prayer ceremony is lit.

Jahaji	Shipmate or fellow traveller. In the West Indies the Indian Immigrants, because of the three-month ocean crossing from India, developed great affection for their shipmates that was maintained long after their indenture was over.
Jamoon	Or jamun and Indian fruit, Jujube.
Jhandi	Literally, flag; a prayer service at the end of which a flag, symbolic of the triumph of good over evil is planted in a consecrated area in the yard.
Kabaka	Slang for African ruler; derogatory.
Kathas	Pujas or religious services at which stories from the ancient texts are retold.
Kailash	The Himalayas, the traditional abode of Shiva.
Kala Pani	Literally the dark water, the oceans which separated the Indian immigrants from India.
Kali	Mother goddess of time, active half of Shiva.
Karilla	Bitter gourd or bitter melon.
Karma	Action, the law of accumulated action and its effects.
Karma Yogi	Person who preforms actions without desire for reward.
Kirtans	Songs in praise of the divine.
Koker	A sluice, from the Dutch.
Laathi	Stick used by Indian stick fighter.
Mamoo	Maternal uncle.
Mandir	Temple.
Maroo	Or mandap; a consecrated and decorated area in which the wedding ceremony takes place.
Murti	Illustration or representation of one of the incarnations of the divine used as an aid to concentration in worship.
Nana	Maternal grandfather.
Nataraja	Shiva in the form of the cosmic dancer; literally the lord of dance.
Neem Margosa	The sacred Indian tree used for a variety of medicinal functions.
Nikka	The wedding ceremony of the Indian Moslem.
Pandit	Hindu priest, learned man.
Panditai	Pandit-hood.

Parabhs	Hindu festive religious observance.
Paramahansa Yogananda	Indian Yogi who founded the Self Realisation Fellowship in Los Angeles 1925 and author of *Autobiography of a Yogi.*
Pranaamed	Greeted with clasped hands.
Phulourie	Indian food made in tiny ball of flour and ground split peas, and fried.
Prasad	Or parsaad, consecrated offering.
Puja	Prayer or prayer ceremony.
Raag	Or raga, a basic Indian musical mode.
Ramayan	The epic historical record of the life of Rama, an incarnation of god. As a living religious text it is second only, perhaps, to the *Mahabharata* among Indians and Hindus in and out of India. the throne but places Rama's slippers on the throne until Rama's return.
Rumaal	Headkerchief, cloth wrapped around woman's head.
Sanaay	To mix food with fingers.
Sarangi	Stringed instrument played like a violin.
Sardar	A chief, a leader, field supervisor.
Shivratri	Celebration of the night of the manifestation of Shiva.
Shiva Lingum	Flame-shaped stone, sometimes called a phallus, representative of Shiva.
Sindhur	Vermilion powder used in Indian religious ceremonies and to make the sacred mark of marriage.
Swami	Person of a spiritual order, or a spiritual leader or ascetic.
Taari	Or tali. Indian brass plate, also used in worship.
Tapasya	Spiritual austerities.

Acknowledgements

The Ontario Arts Council for a Works-In-Progress Award which made possible the completion of this book.

The K M Hunter Foundation and the Ontario Arts Council Foundation for recognising these stories with the 1996 Emerging Artists Award for Literature.

McClelland & Stewart and the judges of the 1997 Journey Prize for selecting, and re-publishing the title story, "Canada Geese and Apple Chatney" in *The Journey Prize Anthology 9: Short Fiction from the Best of Canada's New Writers.*

The Toronto Review, Nurjehan Aziz and M G Vassanji for publishing the title story, "Canada Geese and Apple Chatney", and for the suggestion for the series of linked stories from "S T Writerji".

Mosaic Press and Suwanda Sugunasiri (ed.) for publishing, "When Men Speak This Way" in *The Whistling Thorn: An Anthology of South Asian Canadian Fiction.*

Surface & Symbol and the late Monica Ladell, and *IndiaWorld* and Ronita Torcato for publishing "ST Writerji" in slightly different form.

Peter Nazareth for his encouragement and belief in my work and vision.

Tekilanand and Kshanikadevi and, above all, Sharon for energising . . .

SASENARINE PERSAUD is the author of five books, including the novels *The Ghost of Bellow's Man* (1992) and *Dear Death* (1989), and a book of poetry, *A Surf of Sparrows' Songs* (1996). He is the recipient of the K M Hunter Foundation's Emerging Artist Award for the stories in this collection, and also a Caribbean Heritage Award (1998) for ``outstanding achievements as an author, poet, and literary theorist.'' His work has appeared in publications in Canada, England, India, the Middle East, the United States and the West Indies. One of the stories published here appeared in the 1997 *Journey Prize Anthology* and was a contender for the 1997 Journey Prize. That story was also selected for *The Oxford Book of Caribbean Short Stories*. Persaud was born in Guyana and has lived for several years, until quite recently, in Canada. He is presently based in Florida.